CLASSIC TALES FOR CHILDREN

FUNNY STORIES

CLASSIC TALES FOR CHILDREN
FUNNY STORIES

Compiled and Edited by
TERRY O'BRIEN

RUPA

Published by
Rupa Publications India Pvt. Ltd 2013
161-B/4, Gulmohar House,
Yusuf Sarai Community Centre,
New Delhi 110049

Sales centres:
Bengaluru Chennai
Hyderabad Kolkata Mumbai

P-ISBN: 978-81-291-2453-1
E-ISBN: 978-81-291-2241-4

Seventeenth impression 2026

21 20 19 18 17

Printed in India

Contents

Introduction

Funny Stories is a collection of humourous tales that are great fun to read at any time during the day. The purpose is to tickle your funny bone so you end up laughing out loud!

In *A Trangression,* a collegiate assessor ends up with his love child and knows not what to do with it. Till he realizes it ain't his child at all. But alas! It's already too late!

Meet *The Baron of Grogzwig* who is just too fed up with his married life and wants to end it immediately. But is it going to be that easy?

The Princess and the Puma is all about a young man who wants to woo the princess by killing a Mexican lion. But looks like someone else has already done the job...

A Fishy Story is a classic case of much ado about nothing when a group of three friends realize that the big fish is just a dummy.

A Nose for the King narrates the story of a man who thinks of clearing all his debts by getting the king's nose to do the honours.

My Financial Career is a humorous account of one man's visit to the bank.

Just look at how the *£ The 1,000,000 Bank Notes* gets the whole wide world dancing to the tune of one single man.

And you thought ghosts had no self-esteem of their own! Take a look at *The Canterville Ghost.*

When it comes to *John Mortonson's Funeral,* the last thing everybody wants is to see the man die. But when they peep into his coffin they get a shock of a litetime!

Happy Reading!

A Transgression

Anton Chekhov

A collegiate assessor called Miguev stopped at a telegraph post in the course of his evening walk and heaved a deep sigh. A week before, as he was returning home from his evening walk, he had been overtaken at that very spot by his former housemaid, Agnia, who said to him viciously:

'Wait a bit! I'll cook you such a crab that'll teach you to ruin innocent girls! I'll leave the baby at your door, and I'll have the law of you, and I'll tell your wife, too....'

And she demanded that he should put five thousand roubles into the bank in her name. Miguev remembered it, heaved a sigh, and once more reproached himself with heartfelt repentance for the momentary infatuation which had caused him so much worry and misery.

When he reached his bungalow, he sat down to rest on the doorstep. It was just ten o'clock, and a bit of the moon peeped out from behind the clouds. There was not a soul in the street nor near the bungalows; elderly summer visitors were already going to bed, while young ones were walking in the wood. Feeling in both his pockets for a match to light his cigarette, Miguev brought his elbow into contact with something soft. He looked idly at his right elbow, and his face was instantly contorted by a look of as much horror as though he had seen a snake beside him. On the step at the very door lay a bundle. Something oblong in shape was wrapped up in something—judging by the feel of it, a wadded quilt. One end of the bundle was a little open, and the collegiate assessor, putting in his hand, felt something damp and warm. He leaped on to his feet in horror, and looked about him like a criminal trying to escape from his warders.

'She has left it!' he muttered wrathfully through his teeth, clenching his fists. 'Here it lies... Here lies my transgression! O Lord!'

He was numb with terror, anger, and shame... What was he to do now? What would his wife say if she found out? What would his colleagues at the office say? His Excellency would be sure to dig him in the ribs, guffaw, and say: 'I congratulate you!... He-he-he! Though your beard is grey, your heart is gay... You are a rogue, Semyon Erastovitch!' The whole colony of summer visitors would know his secret now, and probably the respectable mothers of families would shut their doors to him. Such incidents always get into the papers, and the humble name of

Miguev would be published all over Russia…

The middle window of the bungalow was open and he could distinctly hear his wife, Anna Filippovna, laying the table for supper; in the yard close to the gate Yermolay, the porter, was plaintively strumming on the balalaika. The baby had only to wake up and begin to cry, and the secret would be discovered. Miguev was conscious of an overwhelming desire to make haste.

'Haste, haste!…' he muttered, 'this minute, before anyone sees. I'll carry it away and lay it on somebody's doorstep….'

Miguev took the bundle in one hand and quietly, with a deliberate step to avoid awakening suspicion, went down the street….

'A wonderfully nasty position!' he reflected, trying to assume an air of unconcern. 'A collegiate assessor walking down the street with a baby! Good heavens! if anyone sees me and understands the position, I am done for….I'd better put it on this doorstep…. No, stay, the windows are open and perhaps someone is looking. Where shall I put it? I know! I'll take it to the merchant Myelkin's… Merchants are rich people and tenderhearted; very likely they will say thank you and adopt it.'

And Miguev made up his mind to take the baby to Myelkin's, although the merchant's villa was in the furthest street, close to the river.

'If only it does not begin screaming or wriggle

out of the bundle,' thought the collegiate assessor. 'This is indeed a pleasant surprise! Here I am carrying a human being under my arm as though it were a portfolio. A human being, alive, with soul, with feelings like anyone else... If by good luck the Myelkins adopt him, he may turn out somebody... Maybe he will become a professor, a great general, an author... Anything may happen! Now I am carrying him under my arm like a bundle of rubbish, and perhaps in thirty or forty years I may not dare to sit down in his presence...

As Miguev was walking along a narrow, deserted alley, beside a long row of fences, in the thick black shade of the lime trees, it suddenly struck him that he was doing something very cruel and criminal.

'How mean it is really!' he thought. 'So mean that one can't imagine anything meaner... Why are we shifting this poor baby from door to door? It's not its fault that it's been born. It's done us no harm. We are scoundrels... We take our pleasure, and the innocent babies have to pay the penalty. Only to think of all this wretched business! I've done wrong and the child has a cruel fate before it. If I lay it at the Myelkins' door, they'll send it to the foundling hospital, and there it will grow up among strangers, in mechanical routine...no love, no petting, no spoiling... And then he'll be apprenticed to a shoemaker...he'll take to drink, will learn to use filthy language, will go hungry. A shoemaker! and he the son of a collegiate assessor, of good family… He is my flesh and blood…'

Miguev came out of the shade of the lime trees into the bright moonlight of the open road, and opening the bundle, he looked at the baby.

'Asleep!' he murmured. 'You little rascal! why, you've an aquiline nose like your father's.…He sleeps and doesn't feel that its his own father looking at him!…It's a drama, my boy… Well, well, you must forgive me. Forgive me, old boy… It seems it's your fate…'

The collegiate assessor blinked and felt a spasm running down his cheeks… He wrapped up the baby, put him under his arm, and strode on. All the way to the Myelkins' villa social questions were swarming in his brain and conscience was gnawing in his bosom.

'If I were a decent, honest man,' he thought, 'I should damn everything, go with this baby to Anna Filippovna, fall on my knees before her, and say: 'Forgive me! I have sinned! Torture me, but we won't ruin an innocent child. We have no children; let us adopt him!' She's a good sort, she'd consent.… And then my child would be with me… Ech!'

He reached the Myelkins' villa and stood still hesitating. He imagined himself in the parlour at home, sitting reading the paper while a little boy with an aquiline nose played with the tassels of his dressing gown. At the same time visions forced themselves on his brain of his winking colleagues, and of his Excellency digging him in the ribs and guffawing... Besides the pricking of his conscience, there was something warm, sad, and tender in his heart....

Cautiously the collegiate assessor laid the baby on the verandah step and waved his hand. Again he felt a spasm run over his face...

'Forgive me, old fellow! I am a scoundrel, he muttered. 'Don't remember evil against me.'

He stepped back, but immediately cleared his throat resolutely and said:

'Oh, come what will! Damn it all! I'll take him, and let people say what they like!'

Miguev took the baby and strode rapidly back.

'Let them say what they like,' he thought. 'I'll go at once, fall on my knees, and say: 'Anna Filippovna!' Anna is a good sort, she'll understand... And we'll bring him up... If it's a boy we'll call him Vladimir, and if it's a girl we'll call her Anna! Anyway, it will be a comfort in our old age.'

And he did as he determined. Weeping and almost faint with shame and terror, full of hope and vague rapture, he went into his bungalow, went up to his wife, and fell on his knees before her.

'Anna Filippovna!' he said with a sob, and he laid the baby on the floor. 'Hear me before you punish. I have sinned! This is my child... You remember Agnia? Well, it was the devil drove me to it...'

And, almost unconscious with shame and terror, he jumped up without waiting for an answer, and ran out into the open air as though he had received a thrashing....

'I'll stay here outside till she calls me,' he thought. 'I'll give her time to recover, and to think it over...' The porter Yermolay passed him with his balalaika, glanced at him and shrugged his shoulders. A minute later he passed him again, and again he shrugged his shoulders.

'Here's a go! Did you ever!' he muttered grinning. 'Aksinya, the washerwoman, was here just now, Semyon Erastovitch. The silly woman put her baby down on the steps here, and while she was indoors with me, someone took and carried off the baby... Who'd have thought it!'

'What? What are you saying?' shouted Miguev at the top of his voice.

Yermolay, interpreting his master's wrath in his own fashion, scratched his head and heaved a sigh.

'I am sorry, Semyon Erastovitch,' he said, 'but it's the summer holidays...one can't get on without... without a woman, I mean...'

And glancing at his master's eyes glaring at him with anger and astonishment, he cleared his throat guiltily and went on:

'It's a sin, of course, but there—what is one to do? You've forbidden us to have strangers in the house, I know, but we've none of our own now. When Agnia was here I had no women to see me, for I had one at home; but now, you can see for yourself, sir... one can't help having strangers. In Agnia's time, of course, there was nothing irregular, because...'

'Be off, you scoundrel!' Miguev shouted at him, stamping, and he went back into the room.

Anna Filippovna, amazed and wrathful, was sitting as before, her tear-stained eyes fixed on the baby.

'There! there!' Miguev muttered with a pale face, twisting his lips into a smile. 'It was a joke... It's not my baby, it's the washerwoman's!...I...I was joking... Take it to the porter.'

About the Author

Anton Pavlovich Chekhov (29 January 1860 - 15 July 1904) was a Russian physician, dramatist and author who is considered to be among the greatest writers of short stories in history.

The Baron of Grogzwig

Charles Dickens

The Baron Von Koëldwethout, of Grogzwig in Germany, was as likely a young baron as you would wish to see. I needn't say that he lived in a castle, because that's of course; neither need I say that he lived in an old castle; for what German baron ever lived in a new one? There were many strange circumstances connected with this venerable building, among which, not the least startling and mysterious were, that when the wind blew, it rumbled in the chimneys, or even howled among the trees in the neighbouring forest; and that when the moon shone, she found her way through certain small loopholes in the wall, and actually made some parts of the wide halls and galleries quite light, while she left others in gloomy shadow. I believe that one of the baron's ancestors, being short of money, had inserted a dagger in a gentleman who called one night to ask his way, and it was supposed that these miraculous occurrences took place in consequence. And yet I hardly know how that could have been, either, because the baron's ancestor, who was an amiable man, felt very sorry afterwards for having been so rash, and laying violent hands upon a quantity of stone and timber which belonged to a weaker baron, built a chapel as an apology, and so took a receipt from Heaven, in full of all demands.

The Baron Von Koëldwethout of Grogzwig was a fine swarthy fellow, with dark hair and large moustachios, who rode a-hunting in clothes of Lincoln green, with russet boots on his feet, and a bugle slung over his shoulder, like the guard of a long stage. When he blew this bugle, four-and-twenty other gentlemen of inferior rank, in Lincoln green a little coarser, and russet boots with a little thicker soles, turned out directly; and away galloped the whole train, with spears in their hands like lackered area railings, to hunt down the boars, or perhaps encounter a bear, in which latter case the baron killed him first, and greased his whiskers with him afterwards.

This was a merry life for the Baron of Grogzwig, and a merrier still for the baron's retainers, who drank Rhine wine every night till they fell under the table, and then had the bottles on the floor, and called for pipes. Never were such jolly, roystering, rollicking, merry-making blades, as the jovial crew of Grogzwig.

But the pleasures of the table, or the pleasures

of under the table, require a little variety; especially when the same five-and-twenty people sit daily down to the same board, to discuss the same subjects, and tell the same stories. The baron grew weary, and wanted excitement. He took to quarrelling with his gentlemen, and tried kicking two or three of them every day after dinner. This was a pleasant change at first; but it became monotonous after a week or so, and the baron felt quite out of sorts, and cast about, in despair, for some new amusement.

One night, after a day's sport in which he had outdone Nimrod or Gillingwater, and slaughtered 'another fine bear', and brought him home in triumph, the Baron Von Koëldwethout sat moodily at the head of his table, eyeing the smoky roof of the hall with a discontented aspect. He swallowed huge bumpers of wine, but the more he swallowed, the more he frowned. The gentlemen who had been honoured with the dangerous distinction of sitting on his right and left, imitated him to a miracle in the drinking, and frowned at each other.

'I will!' cried the baron suddenly, smiting the table with his right hand, and twirling his moustache with his left. 'Fill to the Lady of Grogzwig!'

The four-and-twenty Lincoln greens turned pale, with the exception of their four-and-twenty noses, which were unchangeable.

'I said to the Lady of Grogzwig,' repeated the baron, looking round the board.

'To the Lady of Grogzwig!' shouted the Lincoln greens; and down their four-and-twenty throats went four-and-twenty imperial pints of such rare old hock, that they smacked their eight-and-forty lips, and winked again.

'The fair daughter of the Baron Von Swillenhausen,' said Koëldwethout, condescending to explain. 'We will demand her in marriage of her father, ere the sun goes down tomorrow. If he refuse our suit, we will cut off his nose.'

A hoarse murmur arose from the company; every man touched, first the hilt of his sword, and then the tip of his nose, with appalling significance.

What a pleasant thing filial piety is, to contemplate! If the daughter of the Baron Von Swillenhausen had pleaded a preoccupied heart, or fallen at her father's feet and corned them in salt tears, or only fainted away, and complimented the old gentleman in frantic ejaculations, the odds are a hundred to one, but Swillenhausen castle would have been turned out at window, or rather the baron turned out at window, and the castle demolished. The damsel held her peace, however, when an early messenger bore the request of Von Koëldwethout next morning, and modestly retired to her chamber, from the casement of which she watched the coming of the suitor and his retinue. She was no sooner assured that the horseman with the large moustachios was her proffered husband, than she hastened to her father's presence, and expressed her readiness to sacrifice herself to secure his peace. The venerable baron caught his child into his arms, and shed a wink of joy.

There was a great feasting at the castle, that day. The four-and-twenty Lincoln greens of Von Koëldwethout exchanged vows of eternal friendship with twelve Lincoln greens of Von Swillenhausen, and promised the old baron that they would drink his wine 'Till all was blue' : meaning probably until their whole countenances had acquired the same tint as their noses. Everybody slapped everybody else's back, when the time for parting came; and the Baron Von Koëldwethout and his followers rode gaily home.

For six mortal weeks, the bears and boars had a holiday. The houses of Koëldwethout and Swillenhausen were united; the spears rusted; and the baron's bugle grew hoarse for lack of blowing.

Those were great times for the four-and-twenty; but, alas! their high and palmy days had taken boots to themselves, and were already walking off.

'My dear,' said the baroness.

'My love,' said the baron.

'Those coarse, noisy men…'

'Which, ma'am?' said the baron starting.

The baroness pointed, from the window at which they stood, to the courtyard beneath, where the unconscious Lincoln greens were taking a copious stirrup-cup, preparatory to issuing forth, after a boar or two.

'My hunting train, ma'am,' said the baron.

'Disband them, love,' murmured the baroness.

'Disband them!' cried the baron, in amazement.

'To please me, love,' replied the baroness.

'To please the devil, ma'am,' answered the baron.

Whereupon the baroness uttered a great cry, and swooned away at the baron's feet.

What could the baron do? He called for the lady's maid, and roared for the doctor; and then, rushing into the yard, kicked the two Lincoln greens who were the most used to it, and cursing the others all round, bade them go, but never mind where, I don't know the German for it, or I would put it delicately that way.

The Baroness Von Koëldwethout somehow or other acquired great control over the Baron Von Koëldwethout, and that, little by little, and bit by bit, and day by day, and year by year, the baron got the worst of some disputed question, or was slyly unhorsed from some old hobby; and that by the time he was a fat hearty fellow of forty-eight or thereabouts, he had no feasting, no revelry, no hunting train, and no hunting, nothing in short that he liked, or used to have; and that, although he was as fierce as a lion and as bold as brass, he was decidedly snubbed and put down, by his own lady, in his own castle of Grogzwig.

Nor was this the whole extent of the baron's misfortunes. About a year after his nuptials, there came into the world a lusty young baron, in whose honour a great many fireworks were let off, and a great many dozens of wine drunk; but next year there came a young baroness, and next year another young baron, and so on, every year, either a baron or baroness (and one year both together), until the baron found himself the father of a small family of twelve. Upon every one of these anniversaries, the venerable Baroness Von Swillenhausen was nervously sensitive for the well-being of her child the Baroness Von Koëldwethout and although it was not found that the good lady ever did anything material towards contributing to her child's recovery, still she made it a point of duty to be as nervous as possible at the castle at Grogzwig, and to divide her time between moral observations on the baron's housekeeping, and bewailing the hard lot of her unhappy daughter.

And if the Baron of Grogzwig, a little hurt and irritated at this, took heart, and ventured to suggest that his wife was at least no worse off than the wives of other barons, the Baroness Von Swillenhausen begged all persons to take notice, that nobody but she, sympathised with her dear daughter's sufferings; upon which, her relations and friends remarked, that to be sure she did cry a great deal more than her son-in-law, and that if there were a hard-hearted brute alive, it was that Baron of Grogzwig.

The poor baron bore it all, as long as he could, and when he could bear it no longer lost his appetite and his spirits, and sat himself gloomily and dejectedly down. But there were worse troubles yet in store for him, and as they came on, his melancholy and sadness increased. Times changed. He got into debt. The Grogzwig coffers ran low, though the Swillenhausen family had looked upon them as inexhaustible; and just when the baroness was on the point of making a thirteenth addition to the family pedigree, Von Koëldwethout discovered that he had no means of replenishing them.

'I don't see what is to be done,' said the baron. 'I think I'll kill myself.'

This was a bright idea. The baron took an old hunting knife from a cupboard hard by, and having sharpened it on his boot, made what boys call 'an offer' at his throat.

'Hem!' said the baron, stopping short. 'Perhaps it's not sharp enough.'

The baron sharpened it again, and made another offer, when his hand was arrested by a loud screaming among the young barons and baronesses, who had a nursery in an upstairs tower with iron bars outside the window, to prevent their tumbling out into the moat.

'If I had been a bachelor,' said the baron sighing, 'I might have done it fifty times over, without being interrupted. Hello! Put a flask of wine and the largest pipe, in the little vaulted room behind the hall.'

One of the domestics, in a very kind manner, executed the baron's order in the course of half an hour or so, and Von Koëldwethout being apprised thereof, strode to the vaulted room, the walls of which, being of dark shining wood, gleamed in the light of the blazing logs which were piled upon the hearth. The bottle and pipe were ready, and, upon the whole, the place looked very comfortable.

'Leave the lamp,' said the baron.

'Anything else, my lord?' inquired the domestic.

'The room,' replied the baron. The domestic obeyed, and the baron locked the door.

'I'll smoke a last pipe,' said the baron, 'and then I'll be off.' So, putting the knife upon the table till he wanted it, and tossing off a goodly measure of wine, the Lord of Grogzwig threw himself back in his chair, stretched his legs out before the fire, and puffed away.

He thought about a great many things... about his present troubles and past days of bachelorship, and about the Lincoln greens, long since disappeared up and down the country, no one knew whither: with the exception of two who had been unfortunately beheaded, and four who had killed themselves with drinking. His mind was running upon bears and boars, when, in the process of draining his glass to the bottom, he raised his eyes, and saw, for the first time and with unbounded astonishment, that he was not alone.

No, he was not; for, on the opposite side of the fire, there sat with folded arms a wrinkled hideous figure, with deeply sunk and bloodshot eyes, and an immensely long, cadaverous face, shadowed by jagged and matted locks of coarse black hair. He wore a kind of tunic of a dull bluish colour, which, the baron observed, on regarding it attentively, was clasped or ornamented down the front, with coffin handles. His legs too, were encased in coffin plates as though in armour; and over his left shoulder he wore a short dusky cloak, which seemed made of remnant of some pall. He took no notice of the baron, but was intently eyeing the fire.

'Halloa!' said the baron, stamping his foot to attract attention.

'Halloa!' replied the stranger, moving his eyes towards the baron, but not his face or himself. 'What now?'

'What now?' replied the baron, nothing daunted by his hollow voice and lustreless eyes, 'I should ask that question. How did you get here?'

'Through the door,' replied the figure.

'What are you?' says the baron.

'A man,' replied the figure.

'I don't believe it,' says the baron.

'Disbelieve it then,' says the figure.

'I will,' rejoined the baron.

The figure looked at the bold Baron of Grogzwig for some time, and then said familiarly,

'There's no coming over you, I see. I'm not a man!'

'What are you then?' asked the baron.

'A genius,' replied the figure.

'You don't look much like one,' returned the baron scornfully.

'I am the Genius of Despair and Suicide,' said the apparition. 'Now you know me.'

With these words the apparition turned towards the baron, as if composing himself for a talk, and, what was very remarkable, was, that he threw his cloak aside, and displaying a stake, which was run through the centre of his body, pulled it out with a jerk, and laid it on the table, as composedly as if it had been a walking stick.

'Now,' said the figure, glancing at the hunting-knife, 'are you ready for me?'

'Not quite,' rejoined the baron; 'I must finish this pipe first.'

'Look sharp then,' said the figure.

You seem in a hurry,' said the baron.

'Why, yes, I am,' answered the figure; 'they're doing a pretty brisk business in my way, over in England and France just now, and my time is a good deal taken up.'

'Do you drink?' said the baron, touching the bottle with the bowl of his pipe.

'Nine times out of ten, and then very hard,' rejoined the figure, dryly.

'Never in moderation?' asked the baron.

'Never,' replied the figure, with a shudder, 'that breeds cheerfulness.'

The baron took another look at his new friend, whom he thought an uncommonly queer customer, and at length inquired whether he took any active part in such little proceedings as that which he had in contemplation.

'No,' replied the figure evasively; 'but I am always present.'

'Just to see fair, I suppose?' said the baron.

'Just that,' replied the figure playing with the stake, and examining the ferule.

'Be as quick as you can, will you, for there's a young gentleman who is afflicted with too much money and leisure wanting me now, I find.'

'Going to kill himself because he has too much money!' exclaimed the baron, quite tickled: 'Ha! ha! that's a good one.' (This was the first time the baron had laughed for many a long day.)

'I say,' expostulated the figure, looking very much scared; 'don't do that again.'

'Why not?' demanded the baron.

'Because it gives me pain all over,' replied the figure. 'Sigh as much as you please; that does me good.'

The baron sighed mechanically, at the mention of the word; the figure, brightening up again, handed him the hunting knife with the most winning politeness.

'It's not a bad idea though,' said the baron, feeling the edge of the weapon; 'a man killing himself because he has too much money.'

'Pooh!' said the apparition, petulantly, 'no better than a man's killing himself because he has none or little.'

Whether the genius unintentionally committed himself in saying this, or whether he thought the baron's mind was so thoroughly made up that it didn't matter what he said, I have no means of knowing. I only know that the baron stopped his hand, all of a sudden, opened his eyes wide, and looked as if quite a new light had come upon him for the first time.

'Why, certainly,' said Von Koëldwethout, 'nothing is too bad to be retrieved.'

'Except empty coffers,' cried the genius.

'Well, but they may be one day filled again,' said the baron.

'Scolding wives,' snarled the genius.

'Oh! They may be made quiet,' said the baron.

'Thirteen children,' shouted the genius.

'Can't all go wrong, surely,' said the baron.

The genius was evidently growing very savage with the baron, for holding these opinions all at once; but he tried to laugh it off, and said if he would let him know when he had left off joking, he should feel obliged to him.

'But I am not joking; I was never farther from it,' remonstrated the baron.

'Well, I am glad to hear that,' said the genius, looking very grim, 'because a joke, without any figure of speech, is the death of me. Come! Quit this dreary world at once.'

'I don't know,' said the baron, playing with the knife; 'it's a dreary one certainly, but I don't think yours is much better, for you have not the appearance of being particularly comfortable. That puts me in mind, that I shall be any the better for going out of the world after all!' he cried, starting up; 'I never thought of that.'

'Dispatch,' cried the figure, gnashing its teeth.

'Keep off!' said the baron, 'I'll brood over miseries no longer, but put a good face on the matter, and try the fresh air and the bears again; and if that don't do, I'll talk to the baroness soundly, and cut the Von Swillenhausens dead.' With this the baron fell into his chair, and laughed so loud and boisterously, that the room rang with it.

The figure fell back a pace or two, regarding the baron meanwhile with a look of intense terror, and when he had ceased, caught up the stake, plunged it violently into its body, uttered a frightful howl, and disappeared.

Von Koëldwethout never saw it again. Having

once made up his mind to action, he soon brought the baroness and the Von Swillenhausens to reason, and died many years afterwards; not a rich man that I am aware of, but certainly a happy one: leaving behind him a numerous family, who had been carefully educated in bear and boar hunting under his own personal eye. And my advice to all men is, that if ever they become hipped and melancholy from similar causes (as very many men do), they look at both sides of the question, applying a magnifying glass to the best one; and if they still feel tempted to retire without leave, that they smoke a large pipe and drink a full bottle first, and profit by the laudable example of the baron of Grogzwig.

About the Author

Charles Dickens (7 February 1812 - 9 June 1870) was an English writer and social critic who is generally regarded as the greatest novelist of the Victorian period, and the creator of some of the world's most memorable fictional characters.

The Princess and Puma

O. Henry

There had to be a king and queen, of course. The king was a terrible old man who wore six-shooters and spurs, and shouted in such a tremendous voice that the rattlers on the prairie would run into their holes under the prickly pear. Before there was a royal family they called the man 'Whispering Ben'. When he came to own 50,000 acres of land and more cattle than he could count, they called him O'Donnell 'the Cattle King.'

The queen had been a Mexican girl from Laredo. She made a good, mild, Colorado wife, and even succeeded in teaching Ben to modify his voice sufficiently while in the house to keep the dishes from being broken. When Ben got to be king she would sit on the gallery of Espinosa Ranch and weave rush mats. When wealth became so irresistible and oppressive that upholstered chairs and a centre table were brought down from San Antone in the wagons, she bowed her smooth, dark head, and shared the fate of the Danaë.

Josefa O'Donnell was the surviving daughter, the princess. From her mother she inherited warmth of nature and a dusky, semi-tropic beauty. From Ben O'Donnell the royal she acquired a store in intrepidity, common sense, and the faculty of ruling. The combination was worth going miles to see. Josefa while riding her pony at a gallop could put five out of six bullets through a tomato can swinging at the end of a string. She could play for hours with a white kitten she owned, dressing it in all manner of absurd clothes. Scorning a pencil, she could tell you out of her head what 1545 two-year-olds would bring on the hoof, at $8.50 per head. Roughly speaking, the Espinosal Ranch is forty miles long and thirty broad—but mostly leased land. Josefa, on her pony, had prospected over every mile of it. Every cow puncher on the range knew her by sight and was a loyal vassal. Ripley Givens, foreman of one of the Espinosal outfits, saw her one day, and made up his mind to form a royal matrimonial alliance. Presumptuous? No. In those days in the Nueces country a man was a man. And, after all, the title of cattle king does not presuppose blood royal. Often it only signifies that its owner wears the crown in token of his magnificent qualities in the art of cattle stealing.

One day Ripley Givens rode over to the Double Elm Ranch to inquire about a bunch of strayed yearlings. He was late in setting out on his return trip, and it was sundown when he struck the White

Horse Crossing of the Nueces. From there to his own camp it was sixteen miles. To the Espinosal ranchhouse it was twelve. Givens was tired. He decided to pass the night at the Crossing.

There was a fine water hole in the river bed. The banks were thickly covered with great trees, undergrown with brush. Back from the water hole fifty yards was a stretch of curly mesquite grass supper for his horse and bed for himself. Givens staked his horse, and spread out his saddle blankets to dry. He sat down with his back against a tree and rolled a cigarette. From somewhere in the dense timber along the river came a sudden, rageful, shivering wail. The pony danced at the end of his rope and blew a whistling snort of comprehending fear. Givens puffed at his cigarette, but he reached leisurely for his pistol belt, which lay on the grass, and twirled the cylinder of his weapon tentatively. A great gar plunged with a loud splash into the water hole. A little brown rabbit skipped around a bunch of catclaw and sat twitching his whiskers and looking humorously at Givens. The pony went on eating grass.

It is well to be reasonably watchful when a Mexican lion sings soprano along the arroyos at sundown. The burden of his song may be that young calves and fat lambs are scarce, and that he has a carnivorous desire for your acquaintance.

In the grass lay an empty fruit can, cast there by some former sojourner. Givens caught sight of it with a grunt of satisfaction. In his coat pocket tied behind his saddle was a handful or two of ground coffee. Black coffee and cigarettes! What ranchero could desire more?

In two minutes he had a little fire going clearly. He started, with his can, for the water hole. When within fifteen yards of its edge he saw, between the bushes, a side-saddled pony with down-dropped reins cropping grass a little distance to his left. Just rising from her hands and knees on the brink of the water hole was Josefa O'Donnell. She had been drinking water, and she brushed the sand from the palms of her hands. Ten yards away, to her right, half concealed by a clump of sacuista, Givens saw the crouching form of the Mexican lion. His amber eyelids glared hungrily; six feet from them was the tip of the tail stretched straight, like a pointer's. His hind-quarters rocked with the motion of the cat tribe preliminary to leaping.

Givens did what he could. His six-shooter was thirty-five yards away lying on the grass. He gave a loud yell, and dashed between the lion and the princess.

The 'rucus', as Givens called it afterward, was brief and somewhat confused. When he arrived on the line of attack he saw a dim streak in the air, and heard a couple of faint cracks. Then a hundred pounds of Mexican lion plumped down upon his head and flattened him, with a heavy jar, to the ground. He remembered calling out: 'Let up, now - no fair gouging!' and then he crawled from under the lion like a worm, with his mouth full of grass and dirt, and a big lump on the back of his head where it had struck the root of a water-elm. The lion lay motionless. Givens, feeling aggrieved, and suspicious of fouls, shook his fist at the lion, and shouted: 'I'll rastle you again for twenty—' and then he got back to himself.

Josefa was standing in her tracks, quietly reloading her silver-mounted .38. It had not been a difficult shot. The lion's head made an easier mark than a tomato-can swinging at the end of a string. There was a provoking, teasing, maddening smile upon her mouth and in her dark eyes. The would-be-rescuing knight felt the fire of his fiasco burn down to his soul. Here had been his chance, the chance that he had dreamed of; and Momus, and not Cupid, had presided over it. The satyrs in the wood were, no doubt, holding their sides in hilarious, silent laughter. There had been something like vaudeville - say Signor Givens and his funny knockabout act with the stuffed lion.

'Is that you, Mr. Givens?' said Josefa, in her deliberate, saccharine contralto. 'You nearly spoiled my shot when you yelled. Did you hurt your head when you fell?'

'Oh, no,' said Givens, quietly; 'that didn't hurt.' He stooped ignominiously and dragged his best

Stetson hat from under the beast. It was crushed and wrinkled to a fine comedy effect. Then he knelt down and softly stroked the fierce, open-jawed head of the dead lion.

'Poor old Bill!' he exclaimed, mournfully.

'What's that?' asked Josefa, sharply.

'Of course you didn't know, Miss Josefa,' said Givens, with an air of one allowing magnanimity to triumph over grief. 'Nobody can blame you. I tried to save him, but I couldn't let you know in time.'

'Save who?'

'Why, Bill. I've been looking for him all day. You see, he's been our camp pet for two years. Poor old fellow, he wouldn't have hurt a cottontail rabbit. It'll break the boys all up when they hear about it. But you couldn't tell, of course, that Bill was just trying to play with you.'

Josefa's black eyes burned steadily upon him. Ripley Givens met the test successfully. He stood rumpling the yellow-brown curls on his head pensively. In his eyes was regret, not unmingled with a gentle reproach. His smooth features were set to a pattern of indisputable sorrow. Josefa wavered.

'What was your pet doing here?' she asked, making a last stand. 'There's no camp near the White Horse Crossing.'

'The old rascal ran away from camp yesterday,' answered Givens, readily. 'It's a wonder the coyotes didn't scare him to death. You see, Jim Webster, our horse wrangler, brought a little terrier pup into camp last week. The pup made life miserable for Bill—he used to chase him around and chew his hind legs for hours at a time. Every night when bedtime came Bill would sneak under one of the boys' blankets and sleep to keep the pup from finding him. I reckon he must have been worried pretty desperate or he wouldn't have run away. He was always afraid to get out of sight of camp.'

Josefa looked at the body of the fierce animal. Givens gently patted one of the formidable paws that could have killed a yearling calf with one blow. Slowly a red flush widened upon the dark olive face of the girl. Was it the signal of shame of the true sportsman who has brought down ignoble quarry? Her eyes grew softer, and the lowered lids drove away all their bright mockery.

'I'm very sorry,' she said, humbly; 'but he looked so big, and jumped so high that—'

'Poor old Bill was hungry,' interrupted Givens, in quick defence of the deceased. 'We always made him jump for his supper in camp. He would lie down and roll over for a piece of meat. When he saw you he thought he was going to get something to eat from you.'

Suddenly Josefa's eyes opened wide.

'I might have shot you!' she exclaimed. 'You ran right in between. You risked your life to save your pet! That was fine, Mr. Givens. I like a man who is kind to animals.'

Yes; there was even admiration in her gaze now. After all, there was a hero rising out of the ruins of the anti-climax. The look on Givens's face would have secured him a high position in the S.P.C.A.

'I always loved 'em,' said he; 'horses, dogs, Mexican lions, cows, alligators—'

'I hate alligators,' instantly demurred Josefa; 'crawly, muddy things!'

'Did I say alligators?' said Givens. 'I meant antelopes, of course.'

Josefa's conscience drove her to make further amends. She held out her hand penitently. There was a bright, unshed drop in each of her eyes.

'Please forgive me, Mr. Givens, won't you? I'm only a girl, you know, and I was frightened at first. I'm very, very sorry I shot Bill. You don't know how ashamed I feel. I wouldn't have done it for anything.'

Givens took the proffered hand. He held it for a time while he allowed the generosity of his nature to overcome his grief at the loss of Bill. At last it was clear that he had forgiven her.

'Please don't speak of it any more, Miss Josefa. 'Twas enough to frighten any young lady the way Bill looked. I'll explain it all right to the boys.'

'Are you really sure you don't hate me?' Josefa came closer to him impulsively. Her eyes were sweet, oh, sweet and pleading with gracious penitence. 'I would hate anyone who would kill my kitten. And how daring and kind of you to risk being shot when you tried to save him! How very few men would have done that!' Victory wrested from defeat! Vaudeville turned into drama! Bravo, Ripley Givens!

It was now twilight. Of course Miss Josefa could not be allowed to ride on to the ranchhouse alone. Givens resaddled his pony in spite of that animal's reproachful glances, and rode with her. Side by side they galloped across the smooth grass, the princess and the man who was kind to animals. The prairie odours of fruitful earth and delicate bloom were thick and sweet around them. Coyotes yelping over there on the hill! No fear. And yet—

Josefa rode closer. A little hand seemed to grope. Givens found it with his own. The ponies kept an even gait. The hands lingered together, and the owner of one explained.

'I never was frightened before, but just think! How terrible it would be to meet a really wild lion! Poor Bill! I'm so glad you came with me!'

O'Donnell was sitting on the ranch gallery

'Hello, Rip!' he shouted - 'that you?'

'He rode in with me,' said Josefa. 'I lost my way and was late.'

'Much obliged,' called the cattle king. 'Stop over, Rip, and ride to camp in the morning.'

But Givens would not. He would push on to camp. There was a bunch of steers to start off on the trail at daybreak. He said goodnight, and trotted away.

An hour later, when the lights were out, Josefa, in her night-robe, came to her door and called to the king in his own room across the brick-paved hallway: 'Say, Pop, you know that old Mexican lion they call the 'Gotch-eared Devil'—the one that killed Gonzales, Mr. Martin's sheep herder, and about fifty calves on the Salada range? Well, I settled his hash this afternoon over at the White Horse Crossing. Put two balls in his head with my .38 while he was on the jump. I knew him by the slice gone from his left ear that old Gonzales cut off with his machete. You couldn't have made a better shot yourself, Daddy.'

'Bully for you!' thundered Whispering Ben from the darkness of the royal chamber.

About The Author

William Sydney Porter (1862 - 1910), known by his pen name O. Henry, was an American writer. O. Henry's short stories are known for their wit, wordplay and clever twist endings.

Mark

H. H. Munro

One morning in December, Augustus Mellowkent sat in his writing room, at work on the third chapter of his eighth novel. He had described at some length, for the benefit of those who could not imagine it, what a rectory garden looks like in July; he was now engaged in describing at greater length the feelings of a young girl, daughter of a long line of rectors and archdeacons, when she discovers for the first time that the postman is attractive.

'Their eyes met, for a brief moment, as he handed her two circulars and the fat wrapper-bound bulk of the East Essex News. Their eyes met, for the merest fraction of a second, yet nothing could ever be quite the same again. Cost what it might, she felt that she must speak, must break the intolerable, unreal silence that had fallen on them. 'How is your mother's rheumatism?' she said.'

The author's labours were cut short by the sudden intrusion of a maidservant.

'A gentleman to see you, sir,' said the maid, handing a card with the name Caiaphas Dwelf inscribed on it; 'says it's important.'

Mellowkent hesitated and yielded; the importance of the visitor's mission was probably illusory, but he had never met anyone with the name Caiaphas before. It would be at least a new experience.

Mr. Dwelf was a man of indefinite age; his high, narrow forehead, cold grey eyes, and determined manner bespoke an unflinching purpose. He had a large book under his arm, and there seemed every probability that he had left a package of similar volumes in the hall. He took a seat before it had been offered him, placed the book on the table, and began to address Mellowkent in the manner of an 'open letter'.

'You are a literary man, the author of several well-known books—'

'I am engaged on a book at the present moment—rather busily engaged,' said Mellowkent, pointedly.

'Exactly,' said the intruder; 'time with you is a commodity of considerable importance. Minutes, even, have their value.'

'They have,' agreed Mellowkent, looking at his watch.

'That,' said Caiaphas, 'is why this book that I am introducing to your notice is not a book that you can afford to be without. 'Right Here' is indispensable for the writing man; it is no ordinary encyclopedia, or I should not trouble to show it to you. It is an inexhaustible mine of concise information—'

'On a shelf at my elbow,' said the author, 'I have a row of reference books that supply me with all the information I am likely to require.'

'Here,' persisted the would-be salesman, 'you have it all in one compact volume. No matter what the subject may be which you wish to look up, or the fact you desire to verify, 'Right Here' gives you all that you want to know in the briefest and most enlightening form. Historical reference, for instance; career of John Huss, let us say. Here we are: 'Huss, John, celebrated religious reformer. Born 1369, burned at Constance 1415. The Emperor Sigismund universally blamed."

'If he had been burnt in these days everyone would have suspected the Suffragettes,' observed Mellowkent.

'Poultry-keeping, now,' resumed Caiaphas, 'that's a subject that might crop up in a novel dealing with English country life. Here we have all about it: 'The Leghorn as egg producer. Lack of maternal instinct in the Minorca. Gapes in chickens, its cause and cure. Ducklings for the early market, how fattened.' There, you see, there it all is, nothing lacking.'

'Except the maternal instinct in the Minorca, and that you could hardly be expected to supply.'

'Sporting records, that's important, too; now how many men, sporting men even, are there who can say offhand what horse won the Derby in any particular year? Now it's just a little thing of that sort—'

'My dear sir,' interrupted Mellowkent, 'there are at least four men in my club who can not only tell me what horse won in any given year, but what horse ought to have won and why it didn't. If your book could supply a method for protecting one from information of that sort it would do more than anything you have yet claimed for it.'

'Geography,' said Caiaphas, imperturbably; 'that's a thing that a busy man, writing at high pressure, may easily make a slip over. Only the other day a well-known author made the Volga flow into the Black Sea instead of the Caspian; now, with this book—'

'On a polished rosewood stand behind you there reposes a reliable and up-to-date atlas,' said Mellowkent; 'and now I must really ask you to be going.'

'An atlas,' said Caiaphas, 'gives merely the chart of the river's course, and indicates the principal towns that it passes. Now 'Right Here' gives you the scenery, traffic, ferry-boat charges, the prevalent types of fish, boatmen's slang terms, and hours of sailing of the principal river steamers. If gives you—'

Mellowkent sat and watched the hard-featured, resolute, pitiless salesman, as he sat doggedly in the chair wherein he had installed himself, unflinchingly extolling the merits of his undesired wares. A spirit of wistful emulation took possession of the author; why could he not live up to the cold stern name he had adopted? Why must he sit here weakly and listen to this weary, unconvincing tirade, why could he not be Mark Mellowkent for a few brief moments, and meet this man on level terms?

A sudden inspiration flashed across his.

'Have you read my last book, *The Cageless Linnet*?' he asked.

'I don't read novels,' said Caiaphas tersely.

'Oh, but you ought to read this one, every one ought to,' exclaimed Mellowkent, fishing the book down from a shelf; 'published at six shillings, you can have it at four-and-six. There is a bit in chapter five that I feel sure you would like, where Emma is alone in the birch copse waiting for Harold Huntingdon—that is the man her family wants her to marry. She really wants to marry him, too, but she does not discover that till chapter fifteen. Listen: 'Far as the eye could stretch rolled the mauve and purple billows of heather, lit up here and there with the glowing yellow of gorse and broom, and edged round with the delicate greys and silver and green of the young birch trees. Tiny blue and brown butterflies fluttered above the fronds of heather, revelling in the sunlight, and overhead the larks were singing as only larks can sing. It was a day when all Nature—' 'In 'Right Here' you have full information on all branches of Nature study,' broke in the bookagent, with a tired note sounding in his voice for the first time; 'forestry, insect life, bird migration, reclamation of waste lands. As I was saying, no man who has to deal with the varied interests of life—'

'I wonder if you would care for one of my earlier books, *The Reluctance of Lady Cullumpton*,' said Mellowkent, hunting again through the bookshelf; 'some people consider it my best novel. Ah, here it is. I see there are one or two spots on the cover, so I won't ask more than three-and-ninepence for it. Do let me read you how it opens:

"Beatrice Lady Cullumpton entered the long, dimly-lit drawing room, her eyes blazing with a hope that she guessed to be groundless, her lips trembling with a fear that she could not disguise. In her hand she carried a small fan, a fragile toy of lace and satinwood. Something snapped as she entered the room; she had crushed the fan into a dozen pieces.'

'There, what do you think of that for an opening? It tells you at once that there's something afoot.'

'I don't read novels,' said Caiaphas sullenly.

'But just think what a resource they are,' exclaimed the author, 'on long winter evenings, or perhaps when you are laid up with a strained ankle—a thing that might happen to anyone; or if you were staying in a house party with persistent wet weather and a stupid hostess and insufferably dull fellow-guests, you would just make an excuse that you had letters to write, go to your room, light a cigarette, and for three-and-ninepence you could plunge into the society of Beatrice Lady Cullumpton and her set. No one ought to travel without one or two of my novels in their luggage as a standby. A friend of mine said only the other day that he would as soon think of going into the tropics without quinine as of going on a visit without a couple of Mark Mellowkents in his kit bag. Perhaps sensation is more in your line. I wonder if I've got a copy of *The Python's Kiss*.'

Caiaphas did not wait to be tempted with selections from that thrilling work of fiction. With a muttered remark about having no time to waste on monkey-talk, he gathered up his slighted volume and departed. He made no audible reply to Mellowkent's cheerful 'Good morning', but the latter fancied that a look of respectful hatred flickered in the cold grey eyes.

About The Author

H. H. Munro (1870 - 1916), better known by the pen name Saki, was a British writer known for his witty, mischievous and sometimes macabre stories.

A Fishy Story
(Three Men in a Boat)

Jerome K. Jerome

We stayed two days at Streatley, and got our clothes washed. We had tried washing them ourselves, in the river, under George's superintendence, and it had been a failure. Indeed, it had been more than a failure, because we were worse off after we had washed our clothes than we were before. Before we had washed them, they had been very, very dirty, it is true; but they were just wearable. After we had washed them—well, the river between Reading and Henley was much cleaner, after we had washed our clothes in it, than it was before. All the dirt contained in the river between Reading and Henley, we collected during that wash, and worked it into our clothes.

The washerwoman at Streatley said she felt she owed it to herself to charge us just three times the usual prices for that wash. She said it had not been like washing, it had been more in the nature of excavating.

We paid the bill without a murmur.

The neighbourhood of Streatley and Goring is a great fishing centre. There is some excellent fishing to be had here. The river abounds in pike, roach, dace, gudgeon, and eels, just here; and you can sit and fish for them all day.

Some people do. They never catch them. I never knew anybody catch anything, up the Thames, except minnows and dead cats, but that has nothing to do, of course, with fishing! The local fisherman's guide doesn't say a word about catching anything. All it says is the place is 'a good station for fishing'; and, from what I have seen of the district, I am quite prepared to bear out this statement.

There is no spot in the world where you can get more fishing, or where you can fish for a longer period. Some fishermen come here and fish for a day, and others stop and fish for a month. You can hang on and fish for a year, if you want to, it will be all the same.

The Angler's Guide to the Thames says that 'jack and perch are also to be had about here', but there *Angler's Guide* is wrong. Jack and perch may be about there. Indeed, I know for a fact that they are. You can see them there in shoals, when you are out for a walk along the banks: they come and stand half out of the water with their mouths open for biscuits.

And, if you go for a bathe, they crowd round, and get in your way, and irritate you. But they are not to be had by a bit of worm on the end of a hook, nor anything like it—not they!

I am not a good fisherman myself. I devoted a considerable amount of attention to the subject at one time, and was getting on, as I thought, fairly well; but the old hands told me that I should never be any real good at it, and advised me to give it up. They said that I was an extremely neat thrower, and that I seemed to have plenty of gumption for the thing, and quite enough constitutional laziness. But they were sure I should never make anything of a fisherman. I had not got sufficient imagination.

They said that as a poet, or a shilling shocker, or a reporter, or anything of that kind, I might be satisfactory, but that, to gain any position as a Thames angler, would require more play of fancy, more power of invention than I appeared to possess.

Some people are under the impression that all that is required to make a good fisherman is the ability to tell lies easily and without blushing; but this is a mistake. Mere bald fabrication is useless; the veriest tyro can manage that. It is in the circumstantial detail, the embellishing touches of probability, the general air of scrupulous—almost of pedantic—veracity, that the experienced angler is seen.

Anybody can come in and say, 'Oh, I caught fifteen

dozen perch yesterday evening'; or 'Last Monday I landed a gudgeon, weighing eighteen pounds, and measuring three feet from the tip to the tail'.

There is no art, no skill, required for that sort of thing. It shows pluck, but that is all.

No; your accomplished angler would scorn to tell a lie, that way. His method is a study in itself.

He comes in quietly with his hat on, appropriates the most comfortable chair, lights his pipe, and commences to puff in silence. He lets the youngsters brag away for a while, and then, during a momentary lull, he removes the pipe from his mouth, and remarks, as he knocks the ashes out against the bars:

'Well, I had a haul on Tuesday evening that it's not much good my telling anybody about.'

'Oh! why's that?' they ask.

'Because I don't expect anybody would believe me if I did,' replies the old fellow calmly, and without even a tinge of bitterness in his tone, as he refills his pipe, and requests the landlord to bring him three of Scotch, cold.

There is a pause after this, nobody feeling sufficiently sure of himself to contradict the old gentleman. So he has to go on by himself without any encouragement.

'No,' he continues thoughtfully; 'I shouldn't believe it myself if anybody told it to me, but it's a fact, for all that. I had been sitting there all the afternoon and had caught literally nothing—except a few dozen dace and a score of jack; and I was just about giving it up as a bad job when I suddenly felt a rather smart pull at the line. I thought it was another little one, and I went to jerk it up. Hang me, if I could move the rod! It took me half-an-hour—half-an-hour, sir!—to land that fish; and every moment I thought the line was going to snap! I reached him at last, and what do you think it was? A sturgeon! a forty pound sturgeon! taken on a line, sir! Yes, you may well look surprised—I'll have another three of Scotch, landlord, please.'

And then he goes on to tell of the astonishment of everybody who saw it; and what his wife said, when he got home, and of what Joe Buggles thought about it.

I asked the landlord of an inn up the river once if it did not injure him, sometimes, listening to the tales that the fishermen about there told him; and he said:

'Oh, no; not now, sir. It did used to knock me over a bit at first, but, lor love you! me and the missus we listens to 'em all day now. It's what you're used to, you know. It's what you're used to.'

I knew a young man once, he was a most conscientious fellow, and when he took to fly-fishing, he determined never to exaggerate his hauls by more than twenty-five per cent.

'When I have caught forty fish,' said he, 'then I

will tell people that I have caught fifty, and so on. But I will not lie any more than that, because it is sinful to lie.'

But the twenty-five per cent plan did not work well at all. He never was able to use it. The greatest number of fish he ever caught in one day was three, and you can't add twenty-five per cent. to three—at least, not in fish.

So he increased his percentage to thirty-three-and-a-third; but that, again, was awkward, when he had only caught one or two; so, to simplify matters, he made up his mind to just double the quantity.

He stuck to this arrangement for a couple of months, and then he grew dissatisfied with it. Nobody believed him when he told them that he only doubled, and he, therefore, gained no credit that way whatever, while his moderation put him at a disadvantage among the other anglers. When he had really caught three small fish, and said he had caught six, it used to make him quite jealous to hear a man, whom he knew for a fact had only caught one, going about telling people he had landed two dozen.

So, eventually, he made one final arrangement with himself, which he has religiously held to ever since, and that was to count each fish that he caught as ten, and to assume ten to begin with. For example, if he did not catch any fish at all, then he said he had caught ten fish—you could never catch less than ten fish by his system; that was the foundation of it. Then, if by any chance he really did catch one fish, he called it twenty, while two fish would count thirty, three forty, and so on.

It is a simple and easily worked plan, and there has been some talk lately of its being made use of by the angling fraternity in general. Indeed, the Committee of the Thames Angler's Association did recommend its adoption about two years ago, but some of the older members opposed it. They said they would consider the idea if the number were doubled, and each fish counted as twenty.

If ever you have an evening to spare, up the river, I should advise you to drop into one of the little village inns, and take a seat in the tap-room. You will be nearly sure to meet one or two old rod-men, sipping their toddy there, and they will tell you enough fishy stories, in half an hour, to give you indigestion for a month.

George and I—I don't know what had become of Harris; he had gone out and had a shave, early in the afternoon, and had then come back and spent full forty minutes in pipeclaying his shoes, we had not seen him since—George and I, therefore, and the dog, left to ourselves, went for a walk to Wallingford on the second evening, and, coming home, we called in at a little riverside inn, for a rest, and other things.

We went into the parlour and sat down. There was an old fellow there, smoking a long clay pipe, and we naturally began chatting.

He told us that it had been a fine day today, and we told him that it had been a fine day yesterday, and then we all told each other that we thought it would be a fine day tomorrow; and George said the crops seemed to be coming up nicely.

After that it came out, somehow or other, that we were strangers in the neighbourhood, and that we were going away the next morning.

Then a pause ensued in the conversation, during which our eyes wandered round the room. They finally rested upon a dusty old glass case, fixed very high up above the chimney piece, and containing a trout. It rather fascinated me, that trout; it was such a monstrous fish. In fact, at first glance, I thought it was a cod.

'Ah!' said the old gentleman, following the direction of my gaze, 'fine fellow that, ain't he?'

'Quite uncommon,' I murmured; and George asked the old man how much he thought it weighed.

'Eighteen pounds six ounces,' said our friend, rising and taking down his coat. 'Yes,' he continued, 'it wur sixteen year ago, come the third o' next month, that I landed him. I caught him just below the bridge with a minnow. They told me he wur in the river, and I said I'd have him, and so I did. You don't see many fish that size about here now, I'm thinking. Good-night, gentlemen, goodnight.'

And out he went, and left us alone.

We could not take our eyes off the fish after that.

It really was a remarkably fine fish. We were still looking at it when the local carrier, who had just stopped at the inn, came to the door of the room with a pot of beer in his hand, and he also looked at the fish.

'Good-sized trout, that,' said George, turning round to him.

'Ah! you may well say that, sir,' replied the man; and then, after a pull at his beer, he added, 'Maybe you wasn't here, sir, when that fish was caught?'

'No,' we told him. We were strangers in the neighbourhood.

'Ah!' said the carrier, 'then, of course, how should you? It was nearly five years ago that I caught that trout.'

'Oh! was it you who caught it, then?' said I.

'Yes, sir,' replied the genial old fellow. 'I caught him just below the lock—leastways, what was the lock then—one Friday afternoon; and the remarkable thing about it is that I caught him with a fly. I'd gone out pike fishing, bless you, never thinking of a trout, and when I saw that whopper on the end of my line, blest if it didn't quite take me aback. Well, you see, he weighed twenty-six pound. Goodnight, gentlemen, goodnight.'

Five minutes afterwards, a third man came in, and described how he had caught it early one morning, with bleak; and then he left, and a stolid, solemn-looking, middle-aged individual came in, and sat down over by the window.

None of us spoke for a while; but, at length, George turned to the newcomer, and said:

'I beg your pardon, I hope you will forgive the liberty that we—perfect strangers in the neighbourhood—are taking, but my friend here and myself would be so much obliged if you would tell us how you caught that trout up there.'

'Why, who told you I caught that trout!' was the surprised query.

We said that nobody had told us so, but somehow or other we felt instinctively that it was he who had done it.

'Well, it's a most remarkable thing—most remarkable,' answered the stolid stranger, laughing; 'because, as a matter of fact, you are quite right. I did catch it. But fancy your guessing it like that. Dear me, it's really a most remarkable thing.'

And then he went on, and told us how it had taken him half an hour to land it, and how it had broken his rod. He said he had weighed it carefully when he reached home, and it had turned the scale at thirty-four pounds.

He went in his turn, and when he was gone, the landlord came in to us. We told him the various histories we had heard about his trout, and he was immensely amused, and we all laughed very heartily.

'Fancy Jim Bates and Joe Muggles and Mr. Jones and old Billy Maunders all telling you that they had caught it. Ha! ha! ha! Well, that is good,' said the honest old fellow, laughing heartily. 'Yes, they are the sort to give it me, to put up in my parlour, if they had caught it, they are! Ha! ha! ha!'

And then he told us the real history of the fish. It seemed that he had caught it himself, years ago, when he was quite a lad; not by any art or skill, but by that unaccountable luck that appears to always wait upon a boy when he plays the wag from school, and goes out fishing on a sunny afternoon, with a bit of string tied on to the end of a tree.

He said that bringing home that trout had saved him from a whacking, and that even his schoolmaster had said it was worth the rule-of-three and practice put together.

He was called out of the room at this point, and George and I again turned our gaze upon the fish.

It really was a most astonishing trout. The more we looked at it, the more we marvelled at it.

It excited George so much that he climbed up on the back of a chair to get a better view of it.

And then the chair slipped, and George clutched wildly at the trout case to save himself, and down it came with a crash, George and the chair on top of it.

'You haven't injured the fish, have you?' I cried in alarm, rushing up.

'I hope not,' said George, rising cautiously and looking about.

But he had. That trout lay shattered into a

thousand fragments—I say a thousand, but they may have only been nine hundred. I did not count them.

We thought it strange and unaccountable that a stuffed trout should break up into little pieces like that.

And so it would have been strange and unaccountable, if it had been a stuffed trout, but it was not.

That trout was plaster-of-Paris.

About The Author

Jerome K. Jerome (2 May 1859 - 14 June 1927) was an English writer and humourist. He is best known for the comic travelogue *Three Men in a Boat* (1889).

A Nose for the King

Jack London

In the morning calm of Korea, when its peace and tranquillity truly merited its ancient name, 'Cho-sen', there lived a politician by name Yi Chin Ho. He was a man of parts, and perhaps in no wise worse than politicians the world over. But, unlike his brethren in other lands, Yi Chin Ho was in jail. Not that he had inadvertently diverted to himself public moneys, but that he had inadvertently diverted too much. Excess is to be deplored in all things, even in grafting, and Yi Chin Ho's excess had brought him to most deplorable straits.

Ten thousand strings of cash he owed the government, and he lay in prison under sentence of death. There was one advantage to the situation—he had plenty of time in which to think. And he thought well. Then called he the jailer to him.

'Most worthy man, you see before you one most wretched,' he began. 'Yet all will be well with me if you will but let me go free for one short hour this night. And all will be well with you, for I shall see to your advancement through the years, and you shall come at length to the directorship of all the prisons of Cho-sen.'

'How, now?' demanded the jailer. 'What foolishness is this? One short hour, and you but waiting for your head to be chopped off! And I, with an aged and much-to-be-respected mother, not to say anything of a wife and several children of tender years! Out upon you for the scoundrel that you are!'

'From the Sacred City to the ends of all the Eight Coasts there is no place for me to hide,' Yi Chin Ho made reply. 'I am a man of wisdom, but of what worth my wisdom here in prison? Were I free, well I know I could seek out and obtain the money wherewith to repay the government. I know of a nose that will save me from all my difficulties.'

'A nose!' cried the jailer.

'A nose,' said Yi Chin Ho. 'A remarkable nose, if I may say so, a most remarkable nose.'

The jailer threw up his hands despairingly. 'Ah, what a wag you are, what a wag,' he laughed. 'To think that that very admirable wit of yours must go the way of the chopping block!'

And so saying, he turned and went away. But in the end, being a man soft of head and heart, when the night was well along he permitted Yi Chin Ho to go.

Straight he went to the Governor, catching him alone and arousing him from his sleep.

'Yi Chin Ho, or I'm no Governor!' cried the Governor. 'What do you here who should be in prison waiting on the chopping block?'

'I pray your excellency to listen to me,' said Yi Chin Ho, squatting on his hams by the bedside and lighting his pipe from the fire box. 'A dead man is without value. It is true, I am as a dead man, without value to the government, to your excellency, or to myself. But if, so to say, your excellency were to give me my freedom—'

'Impossible!' cried the Governor. 'Besides, you are condemned to death.'

'Your excellency well knows that if I can repay the ten thousand strings of cash, the government will pardon me,' Yi Chin Ho went on. 'So, as I say, if your excellency were to give me my freedom for a few days, being a man of understanding, I should then repay the government and be in position to be of service to your excellency. I should be in position to be of very great service to your excellency.'

'Have you a plan whereby you hope to obtain this money?' asked I the Governor.

'I have,' said Yi Chin Ho.

'Then come with it to me tomorrow night; I would now sleep,' said the Governor, taking up his snore where it had been interrupted.

On the following night, having again obtained leave of absence from the jailer, Yi Chin Ho presented himself at the Governor's bedside.

'Is it you, Yi Chin Ho?' asked the Governor. 'And have you the plan?'

'It is I, your excellency,' answered Yi Chin Ho, 'and the plan is here.'

'Speak,' commanded the Governor.

'The plan is here,' repeated Yi Chin Ho, 'here in my hand.'

The Governor sat up and opened his eyes. Yi Chin Ho proffered in his hand a sheet of paper. The Governor held it to the light.

'Nothing but a nose,' said he.

'A bit pinched, so, and so, your excellency,' said Yi Chin Ho.

'Yes, a bit pinched here and there, as you say,' said the Governor.

'Withal it is an exceeding corpulent nose, thus, and so, all in one place, at the end,' proceeded Yi Chin Ho. 'Your excellency would seek far and wide and many a day for that nose and find it not.'

'An unusual nose,' admitted the Governor.

'There is a wart upon it,' said Yi Chin Ho.

'A most unusual nose,' said the Governor. 'Never have I seen the like. But what do you with this nose, Yi Chin Ho?'

'I seek it whereby to repay the money to the government,' said Yi Chin Ho. 'I seek it to be of service to your excellency, and I seek it to save my own worthless head. Further, I seek your excellency's seal upon this picture of the nose.'

And the Governor laughed and affixed the seal of state, and Yi Chin Ho departed. For a month and a day he travelled the King's Road which leads to the shore of the Eastern Sea; and there, one night, at the gate of the largest mansion of a wealthy city he knocked loudly for admittance.

'None other than the master of the house will I see,' said he fiercely to the frightened servants. 'I travel upon the King's business.'

Straightway was he led to an inner room, where the master of the house was roused from his sleep and brought blinking before him.

'You are Pak Chung Chang, head man of this city,' said Yi Chin Ho in tones that were all-accusing. 'I am upon the King's business.'

Pak Chung Chang trembled. Well he knew the King's business was ever a terrible business. His knees smote together, and he near fell to the floor.

'The hour is late,' he quavered. 'Were it not well to—'

'The King's business never waits!' thundered Yi Chin Ho. 'Come apart with me, and swiftly. I have an affair of moment to discuss with you.

'It is the King's affair,' he added with even greater fierceness; so that Pak Chung Chang's silver pipe dropped from his nerveless fingers and clattered on the floor.

'Know then,' said Yi Chin Ho, when they had gone apart, 'that the King is troubled with an affliction, a very terrible affliction. In that he failed to cure, the Court physician has had nothing else than his head chopped off. From all the Eight Provinces have the physicians come to wait upon the King. Wise consultation have they held, and they have decided that for a remedy for the King's affliction nothing else is required than a nose, a certain kind of nose, a very peculiar certain kind of nose.

'Then by none other was I summoned than his excellency the prime minister himself. He put a paper into my hand. Upon this paper was the very peculiar kind of nose drawn by the physicians of the Eight Provinces, with the seal of state upon it.

"Go,' said his excellency the prime minister. 'Seek out this nose, for the King's affliction is sore. And wheresoever you find this nose upon the face of a man, strike it off forthright and bring it in all haste to the Court, for the King must be cured. Go, and come not back until your search is rewarded.'

'And so I departed upon my quest,' said Yi Chin Ho. 'I have sought out the remotest corners of the kingdom; I have travelled the Eight Highways, searched the Eight Provinces, and sailed the seas of the Eight Coasts. And here I am.'

With a great flourish he drew a paper from his girdle, unrolled it with many snappings and cracklings, and thrust it before the face of Pak Chung Chang. Upon the paper was the picture of the nose.

Pak Chung Chang stared upon it with bulging eyes.

'Never have I beheld such a nose,' he began.

'There is a wart upon it,' said Yi Chin Ho.

'Never have I beheld—' Pak Chung Chang began again.

'Bring your father before me,' Yi Chin Ho interrupted sternly.

'My ancient and very-much-to-be-respected ancestor sleeps,' said Pak Chung Chang.

'Why dissemble?' demanded Yi Chin Ho. 'You know it is your father's nose. Bring him before me that I may strike it off and be gone. Hurry, lest I make bad report of you.'

'Mercy!' cried Pak Chung Chang, falling on his knees. 'It is impossible! It is impossible! You cannot strike off my father's nose. He cannot go down without his nose to the grave. He will become a laughter and a byword, and all my days and nights will be filled with woe. O reflect! Report that you have seen no such nose in your travels. You, too, have a father.'

Pak Chung Chang clasped Yi Chin Ho's knees and fell to weeping on his sandals.

'My heart softens strangely at your tears,' said Yi Chin Ho. 'I, too, know filial piety and regard. But—' He hesitated, then added, as though thinking aloud, 'It is as much as my head is worth.'

'How much is your head worth ?' asked Pak Chung Chang in a thin, small voice.

'A not remarkable head,' said Yi Chin Ho. 'An absurdly unremarkable head; but, such is my great foolishness, I value it at nothing less than one hundred thousand strings of cash.'

'So be it,' said Pak Chung Chang, rising to his feet.

'I shall need horses to carry the treasure,' said Yi Chin Ho, 'and men to guard it well as I journey through the mountains. There are robbers abroad in the land.'

'There are robbers abroad in the land,' said Pak Chung Chang, sadly. 'But it shall be as you wish, so long as my ancient and very-much-to-be-respected ancestor's nose abide in its appointed place.'

'Say nothing to any man of this occurrence,' said Yi Chin Ho, 'else will other and more loyal servants than I be sent to strike off your father's nose.'

And so Yi Chin Ho departed on his way through the mountains, blithe of heart and gay of song as he listened to the jingling bells of his treasure-laden ponies.

There is little more to tell. Yi Chin Ho prospered through the years. By his efforts the jailer attained at length to the directorship of all the prisons of Cho-sen; the Governor ultimately betook himself to the Sacred City to be prime minister to the King, while Yi Chin Ho became the King's boon companion and sat at table with him to the end of a round, fat life. But Pak Chung Chang fell into a melancholy, and ever after he shook his head sadly, with tears in his eyes, whenever he regarded the expensive nose of his ancient and very-much-to-be-respected ancestor.

About The Author

John 'Jack' London (January 12, 1876 – November 22, 1916) was an American author, journalist, and social activist. He was one of the first fiction writers to obtain worldwide celebrity and a large fortune from his fiction alone.

My Financial Career

Stephen Leacock

When I go into a bank I get rattled. The clerks rattle me; the wickets rattle me; the sight of the money rattles me; everything rattles me. The moment I cross the threshold of a bank and attempt to transact business there, I become an irresponsible idiot.

I knew this beforehand, but my salary had been raised to fifty dollars a month and I felt that the bank was the only place for it. So I shambled in and looked timidly round at the clerks. I had an idea that a person about to open an account must needs consult the manager.

I went up to a wicket marked 'Accountant.' The accountant was a tall, cool devil. The very sight of him rattled me. My voice was sepulchral.

'Can I see the manager?' I said, and added solemnly, 'alone.' I don't know why I said 'alone'.

'Certainly,' said the accountant, and fetched him. The manager was a grave, calm man. I held my fifty-six dollars clutched in a crumpled ball in my pocket.

'Are you the manager?' I said. God knows I didn't doubt it.

'Yes,' he said.

'Can I see you,' I asked, 'alone?' I didn't want to say 'alone' again, but without it the thing seemed self-evident.

The manager looked at me in some alarm. He felt that I had an awful secret to reveal.

'Come in here,' he said, and led the way to a private room. He turned the key in the lock.

'We are safe from interruption here,' he said. 'Sit down.'

We both sat down and looked at each other. I found no voice to speak.

'You are one of Pinkerton's men, I presume,' he said.

He had gathered from my mysterious manner that I was a detective. I knew what he was thinking, and it made me worse.

'No, not from Pinkerton's,' I said, seeming to imply that I came from a rival agency.

'To tell the truth,' I went on, as if I had been prompted to lie about it, 'I am not a detective at all. I have come to open an account. I intend to keep all my money in this bank.'

The manager looked relieved but still serious; he concluded now that I was a son of Baron Rothschild or a young Gould.

'A large account, I suppose,' he said.

'Fairly large,' I whispered. 'I propose to deposit fifty-six dollars now and fifty dollars a month regularly.'

The manager got up and opened the door. He called to the accountant.

'Mr Montgomery,' he said, unkindly loud, 'this gentleman is opening an account, he will deposit fifty-six dollars. Good morning.'

I rose.

A big iron door stood open at the side of the room.

'Good morning,' I said, and stepped into the safe.

'Come out,' said the manager coldly, and showed me the other way.

I went up to the accountant's wicket and poked the ball of money at him with a quick convulsive movement as if I were doing a conjuring trick.

My face was ghastly pale.

'Here,' I said, 'deposit it.' The tone of the words seemed to mean, 'Let us do this painful thing while the fit is on us.'

He took the money and gave it to another clerk.

He made me write the sum on a slip and sign my name in a book. I no longer knew what I was doing. The bank swam before my eyes.

'Is it deposited?' I asked in a hollow, vibrating voice.

'It is,' said the accountant.

'Then I want to draw a cheque.' My idea was to

draw out six dollars of it for present use. Someone gave me a cheque book through a wicket and someone else began telling me how to write it out. The people in the bank had the impression that I was an invalid millionaire. I wrote something on the cheque and thrust it in at the clerk. He looked at it.

'What! Are you drawing it all out again?' he asked in surprise. Then I realized that I had written fifty-six instead of six. I was too far gone to reason now. I had a feeling that it was impossible to explain the thing. All the clerks had stopped writing to look at me.

Reckless with misery, I made a plunge.

'Yes, the whole thing.'

'You withdraw your money from the bank?'

'Every cent of it.'

'Are you not going to deposit any more?' said the clerk, astonished.

'Never.'

An idiot hope struck me that they might think something had insulted me while I was writing the cheque and that I had changed my mind. I made a wretched attempt to look like a man with a fearfully quick temper.

The clerk prepared to pay the money.

'How will you have it?' he said.

'What?'

'How will you have it?'

'Oh,' I caught his meaning and answered without

even trying to think, 'in fifties.'

He gave me a fifty-dollar bill. 'And the six?' he asked dryly.

'In sixes,' I said.

He gave it me and I rushed out.

As the big door swung behind me, I caught the echo of a roar of laughter that went up to the ceiling of the bank. Since then I bank no more. I keep my money in cash in my trousers pocket and my savings in silver dollars in a sock.

About the Author

Stephen Butler Leacock (30 December 1869–28 March 1944) was an English-born Canadian teacher, political scientist, writer and humorist.

The £1,000,000 Bank-Note

Mark Twain

When I was twenty-seven years old, I was a mining broker's clerk in San Francisco, and an expert in all the details of stock traffic. I was alone in the world, and had nothing to depend upon but my wits and a clean reputation; but these were setting my feet in the road to eventual fortune, and I was content with the prospect.

My time was my own after the afternoon board, Saturdays, and I was accustomed to put it in on a little sailboat on the bay. One day I ventured too far, and was carried out to sea. Just at nightfall, when hope was about gone, I was picked up by a small brig which was bound for London. It was a long and stormy voyage, and they made me work my passage without pay, as a common sailor. When I stepped ashore in London my clothes were ragged and shabby, and I had only a dollar in my pocket.

This money fed and sheltered me twenty-four hours. During the next twenty-four I went without food and shelter.

About ten o'clock on the following morning, seedy and hungry, I was dragging myself along Portland Place, when a child that was passing, towed by a nurse—maid, tossed a luscious big pear—minus one bite—into the gutter. I stopped, of course, and fastened my desiring eye on that muddy treasure. My mouth watered for it, my stomach craved it, my whole being begged for it. But every time I made a move to get it some passing eye detected my purpose, and of course I straightened up then, and looked indifferent, and pretended that I hadn't been thinking about the pear at all. This same thing kept happening and happening, and I couldn't get the pear. I was just getting desperate enough to brave all the shame, and to seize it, when a window behind me was raised, and a gentleman spoke out of it, saying:

'Step in here, please.'

I was admitted by a gorgeous flunkey, and shown into a sumptuous room where a couple of elderly gentlemen were sitting. They sent away the servant, and made me sit down. They had just finished their breakfast, and the sight of the remains of it almost overpowered me. I could hardly keep my wits together in the presence of that food, but as I was not asked to sample it, I had to bear my trouble as best I could.

Now, something had been happening there a little before, which I did not know anything about until a good many days afterwards, but I will tell you about it now. Those two old brothers had been having a pretty hot argument a couple of days before, and had ended by agreeing to decide it by a bet, which is the English way of settling everything.

You will remember that the Bank of England once issued two notes of a million pounds each, to be used for a special purpose connected with some public transaction with a foreign country. For some reason or other only one of these had been used and cancelled; the other still lay in the vaults of the Bank. Well, the brothers, chatting along, happened to get to wondering what might be the fate of a perfectly honest and intelligent stranger who should be turned adrift in London without a friend, and with no money but that million-pound bank-note, and no way to account for his being in possession of it. Brother A said he would starve to death; Brother B said he wouldn't. Brother A said he couldn't offer it at a bank or anywhere else, because he would be arrested on the spot. So they went on disputing till Brother B said he would bet twenty thousand pounds that the man would live thirty days, anyway, on that million, and keep out of jail, too. Brother A took him up. Brother B went down to the Bank and bought that note. Just like an Englishman, you see; pluck to the backbone. Then he dictated a letter, which one of his clerks wrote out in a beautiful round hand, and then the two brothers sat at the window a whole day watching for the right man to give it to.

They saw many honest faces go by that were not intelligent enough; many that were intelligent, but not honest enough; many that were both, but the possessors were not poor enough, or, if poor enough, were not strangers. There was always a defect, until I came along; but they agreed that I filled the bill all around; so they elected me unanimously, and there I was now waiting to know why I was called in. They began to ask me questions about myself, and pretty soon they had my story. Finally they told me I would answer their purpose. I said I was sincerely glad, and asked what it was. Then one of them handed me an envelope, and said I would find the explanation inside. I was going to open it, but he said no; take it to my lodgings, and look it over carefully, and not be hasty or rash. I was puzzled, and wanted to discuss the matter a little further, but they didn't; so I took my leave, feeling hurt and insulted to be made the butt of what was apparently some kind of a practical joke, and yet obliged to put up with it, not being in circumstances to resent affronts from rich and strong folk.

I would have picked up the pear now and eaten it before all the world, but it was gone; so I had lost that by this unlucky business, and the thought of it did not soften my feeling towards those men. As soon as I was out of sight of that house I opened my envelope, and saw that it contained money! My opinion of those people changed, I can tell you! I lost not a moment, but shoved note and money into my vest pocket, and broke for the nearest cheap eating house. Well, how I did eat! When at last I couldn't hold any more, I took out my money and unfolded it, took one glimpse and nearly fainted. Five millions of dollars! Why, it made my head swim.

I must have sat there stunned and blinking at the note as much as a minute before I came rightly to myself again. The first thing I noticed, then, was the landlord. His eye was on the note, and he was petrified. He was worshiping, with all his body and soul, but he looked as if he couldn't stir hand or foot. I took my cue in a moment, and did the only rational thing there was to do. I reached the note towards him, and said, carelessly:

'Give me the change, please.'

Then he was restored to his normal condition, and made a thousand apologies for not being able to break the bill, and I couldn't get him to touch it. He wanted to look at it, and keep on looking at it; he couldn't seem to get enough of it to quench the thirst of his eye, but he shrank from touching it as if it had been something too sacred for poor common clay to handle. I said:

'I am sorry if it is an inconvenience, but I must insist. Please change it; I haven't anything else.'

But he said that wasn't any matter; he was quite willing to let the trifle stand over till another time. I said I might not be in his neighborhood again for a good while; but he said it was of no consequence, he could wait, and, moreover, I could have anything I wanted, any time I chose, and let the account run as long as I pleased. He said he hoped he wasn't afraid to trust as rich a gentleman as I was, merely because I was of a merry disposition, and chose to play larks on the public in the matter of dress. By this time another customer was entering, and the landlord hinted to me to put the monster out of sight; then he bowed me all the way to the door, and I started straight for that house and those brothers, to correct the mistake which had been made before the police should hunt me up, and help me do it. I was pretty nervous; in fact, pretty badly frightened, though, of course, I was no way in fault; but I knew men well enough to know that when they find they've given a tramp a million-pound bill when they thought it was a one-pounder, they are in a frantic rage against him instead of quarreling with their own near-sightedness, as they ought. As I approached the house my excitement began to abate, for all was quiet there, which made me feel pretty sure the blunder was not discovered yet. I rang. The same servant appeared. I asked for those gentlemen.

'They are gone.' This in the lofty, cold way of that fellow's tribe.

'Gone? Gone where?'

'On a journey.'

'But whereabouts?'

'To the Continent, I think.'

'The Continent?'

'Yes, sir.'

'Which way—by what route?'

'I can't say, sir.'

'When will they be back?'

'In a month, they said.'

'A month! Oh, this is awful! Give me some sort of idea of how to get a word to them. It's of the last importance.'

'I can't, indeed. I've no idea where they've gone, sir.'

'Then I must see some member of the family.'

'Family's away, too; been abroad months—in Egypt and India, I think.'

'Man, there's been an immense mistake made. They'll be back before night. Will you tell them I've been here, and that I will keep coming till it's all made right, and they needn't be afraid?'

'I'll tell them, if they come back, but I am not expecting them. They said you would be here in an hour to make inquiries, but I must tell you it's all right, they'll be here on time and expect you.'

So I had to give it up and go away. What a riddle it all was! I was like to lose my mind. They would be here 'on time'. What could that mean? Oh, the letter would explain, maybe. I had forgotten the letter; I got it out and read it. This is what it said:

'You are an intelligent and honest man, as one may see by your face. We conceive you to be poor and a stranger. Enclosed you will find a sum of money. It is lent to you for thirty days, without interest. Report at this house at the end of that time. I have a bet on you. If I win it you shall have any situation that is in my gift—any, that is, that you shall be able to prove yourself familiar with and competent to fill.'

No signature, no address, no date.

Well, here was a coil to be in! You are posted on what had preceded all this, but I was not. It was just a deep, dark puzzle to me. I hadn't the least idea what the game was, nor whether harm was meant me or a kindness. I went into a park, and sat down to try to think it out, and to consider what I had best do.

At the end of an hour my reasonings had crystallised into this verdict.

Maybe those men mean me well, maybe they mean me ill; no way to decide that—let it go. They've got a game, or a scheme, or an experiment, of some kind on hand; no way to determine what it is—let it go. There's a bet on me; no way to find out what it is—let it go. That disposes of the indeterminable quantities; the remainder of the matter is tangible, solid, and may be classed and labelled with certainty. If I ask the Bank of England to place this bill to the credit of the man it belongs to, they'll do it, for they know him, although I don't; but they will ask me how I came in possession of it, and if I tell the truth, they'll put me in the asylum, naturally, and a lie will land me in jail. The same result would follow if I tried to bank the bill anywhere or to borrow money on it. I have got to carry this immense burden around until those men come back, whether I want to or not. It is useless to me, as useless as a handful of ashes, and yet I must take care of it, and watch over it, while I beg my living. I couldn't give it away, if I should try, for neither honest citizen nor highwayman would accept it or meddle with it for anything. Those brothers are safe. Even if I lose their bill, or burn it, they are still safe, because they can stop payment, and the Bank will make them whole; but meantime I've got to do a month's suffering without wages or profit—unless I help win that bet, whatever it may be, and get that situation that I am promised. I should like to get that; men of their sort have situations in their gift that are worth having.

I got to thinking a good deal about that situation. My hopes began to rise high. Without doubt the salary would be large. It would begin in a month; after that I should be all right. Pretty soon I was feeling first-rate. By this time I was tramping the streets again. The sight of a tailor shop gave me a sharp longing to shed my rags, and to clothe myself decently once more. Could I afford it? No; I had nothing in the world but a million pounds. So

I forced myself to go on by. But soon I was drifting back again. The temptation persecuted me cruelly. I must have passed that shop back and forth six times during that manful struggle. At last I gave in; I had to. I asked if they had a misfit suit that had been thrown on their hands. The fellow I spoke to nodded his head towards another fellow, and gave me no answer. I went to the indicated fellow, and he indicated another fellow with his head, and no words. I went to him, and he said:

'Tend to you presently.'

I waited till he was done with what he was at, then he took me into a back room, and overhauled a pile of rejected suits, and selected the rattiest one for me. I put it on. It didn't fit, and wasn't in any way attractive, but it was new, and I was anxious to have it; so I didn't find any fault, but said, with some diffidence:

'It would be an accommodation to me if you could wait some days for the money. I haven't any small change about me.'

The fellow worked up a most sarcastic expression of countenance, and said:

'Oh, you haven't? Well, of course, I didn't expect it. I'd only expect gentlemen like you to carry large change.'

I was nettled, and said:

'My friend, you shouldn't judge a stranger always by the clothes he wears. I am quite able to pay for this suit; I simply didn't wish to put you to the trouble of changing a large note.'

He modified his style a little at that, and said, though still with something of an air:

'I didn't mean any particular harm, but as long as rebukes are going, I might say it wasn't quite your affair to jump to the conclusion that we couldn't change any note that you might happen to be carrying around. On the contrary, we can.'

I handed the note to him, and said:

'Oh, very well; I apologise.'

He received it with a smile, one of those large smiles which goes all around over, and has folds in it, and wrinkles, and spirals, and looks like the place where you have thrown a brick in a pond; and then in the act of his taking a glimpse of the bill this smile froze solid, and turned yellow, and looked like those wavy, wormy spreads of lava which you find hardened on little levels on the side of Vesuvius. I never before saw a smile caught like that, and perpetuated. The man stood there holding the bill, and looking like that, and the proprietor hustled up to see what was the matter, and said, briskly:

'Well, what's up? What's the trouble? What's wanting?'

I said: 'There isn't any trouble. I'm waiting for my change.'

'Come, come; get him his change, Tod; get him his change.'

Tod retorted: 'Get him his change! It's easy to say, sir; but look at the bill yourself.'

The proprietor took a look, gave a low, eloquent whistle, then made a dive for the pile of rejected clothing, and began to snatch it this way and that, talking all the time excitedly, and as if to himself:

'Sell an eccentric millionaire such an unspeakable suit as that! Tod's a fool—a born fool. Always doing something like this. Drives every millionaire away from this place, because he can't tell a millionaire from a tramp, and never could. Ah, here's the thing I am after. Please get those things off, sir, and throw them in the fire. Do me the favour to put on this shirt and this suit; it's just the thing, the very thing—plain, rich, modest, and just ducally nobby; made to order for a foreign prince—you may know him, sir, his Serene Highness the Hospodar of Halifax; had to leave it with us and take a mourning-suit because his mother was going to die—which she didn't. But that's all right; we can't always have things the way we—that is, the way they—there! trousers all right, they fit you to a charm, sir; now the waistcoat; aha, right again! now the coat—Lord! look at that, now! Perfect—the whole thing! I never saw such a triumph in all my experience.'

I expressed my satisfaction.

'Quite right, sir, quite right; it'll do for a makeshift, I'm bound to say. But wait till you see what we'll get up for you on your own measure. Come, Tod, book and pen; get at it. Length of leg, 32" and so on. Before I could get in a word he had measured me, and was giving orders for dress-suits, morning suits, shirts, and all sorts of things. When I got a chance I said:

'But, my dear sir, I can't give these orders, unless you can wait indefinitely, or change the bill.'

'Indefinitely! It's a weak word, sir, a weak word. Eternally - that's the word, sir. Tod, rush these things through, and send them to the gentleman's address without any waste of time. Let the minor customers wait. Set down the gentleman's address and—'

'I'm changing my quarters. I will drop in and leave the new address.'

'Quite right, sir, quite right. One moment—let me show you out, sir. There—good day, sir, good day.'

Well, don't you see what was bound to happen? I drifted naturally into buying whatever I wanted, and asking for change. Within a week I was sumptuously equipped with all needful comforts and luxuries, and was housed in an expensive private hotel in Hanover Square. I took my dinners there, but for breakfast I stuck by Harris's humble feeding house, where I had got my first meal on my million-pound bill. I was the making of Harris. The fact had gone all abroad that the foreign crank who carried million-pound bills in his vest pocket was the patron saint of the place. That was enough. From being a poor, struggling, little hand-to-mouth enterprise, it had become celebrated, and overcrowded with customers. Harris was so grateful that he forced loans upon me, and would not be denied; and so, pauper as I was, I had money to spend, and was living like the rich and the great. I judged that there was going to be a crash by and by, but I was in now and must swim across or drown. You see there was just that element of impending disaster to give a serious side, a sober side, yes, a tragic side, to a state of things which would otherwise have been purely ridiculous. In the night, in the dark, the tragedy part was always to the front, and always warning, always threatening; and so I moaned and tossed, and sleep was hard to find. But in the cheerful daylight the tragedy element faded out and disappeared, and I walked on air, and was happy to giddiness, to intoxication, you may say.

And it was natural; for I had become one of the notorieties of the metropolis of the world, and it turned my head, not just a little, but a good deal. You could not take up a newspaper, English, Scotch, or Irish, without finding in it one or more references to the 'vest-pocket million-pounder' and his latest doings and saying. At first, in these mentions, I was at the bottom of the personal-gossip column; next, I was listed above the knights, next above the baronets, next above the barons, and so on, and so on, climbing steadily, as my notoriety augmented, until I reached the highest altitude possible, and there I remained, taking precedence of all dukes not royal, and of all ecclesiastics except the primate of all England. But mind, this was not fame; as yet I had achieved only notoriety. Then came the climaxing stroke—the accolade, so to speak—which in a single instant transmuted the perishable dross of notoriety into the enduring gold of fame: *Punch* caricatured me! Yes, I was a made man now; my place was established. I might be joked about still, but reverently, not hilariously, not rudely; I could be smiled at, but not laughed at. The time for that had gone by. *Punch* pictured me all a-flutter with rags, dickering with a beef-eater for the Tower of London. Well, you can imagine how it was with a young fellow who had never been taken notice of before, and now all of a sudden couldn't say a thing that wasn't taken up and repeated everywhere; couldn't stir abroad without constantly overhearing the remark flying from lip to lip, 'There he goes; that's him!' couldn't take his breakfast without a crowd to look on; couldn't appear in an operabox without concentrating there the fire of a thousand lorgnettes. Why, I just swam in glory all day long—that is the amount of it.

You know, I even kept my old suit of rags, and every now and then appeared in them, so as to have the old pleasure of buying trifles, and being insulted, and then shooting the scoffer dead with the million-pound bill. But I couldn't keep that up. The illustrated papers made the outfit so familiar that when I went out in it I was at once recognized and followed by a crowd, and if I attempted a purchase the man would offer me his whole shop on credit before I could pull my note on him.

About the tenth day of my fame I went to fulfil my duty to my flag by paying my respects to the American minister. He received me with the enthusiasm proper in my case, upbraided me for being so tardy in my duty, and said that there was only one way to get his forgiveness, and that was to take the seat at his dinner party that night made vacant by the illness of one of his guests. I said I would, and we got to talking. It turned out that he and my father had been schoolmates in boyhood, Yale students together later, and always warm friends up to my father's death. So then he required me to put in at his house all the odd time I might have to spare, and I was very willing, of course.

In fact, I was more than willing; I was glad. When the crash should come, he might somehow be able to save me from total destruction; I didn't know how, but he might think of a way, maybe. I couldn't venture to unbosom myself to him at this late date, a thing which I would have been quick to do in the beginning of this awful career of mine in London. No, I couldn't venture it now; I was in too deep; that is, too deep for me to be risking revelations to so new a friend, though not clear beyond my depth, as I looked at it. Because, you see, with all my borrowing,

I was carefully keeping within my means—I mean within my salary. Of course, I couldn't know what my salary was going to be, but I had a good enough basis for an estimate in the fact, that if I won the bet I was to have choice of any situation in that rich old gentleman's gift provided I was competent—and I should certainly prove competent; I hadn't any doubt about that. And as to the bet, I wasn't worrying about that; I had always been lucky. Now my estimate of the salary was six hundred to a thousand a year; say, six hundred for the first year, and so on up year by year, till I struck the upper figure by proved merit. At present I was only in debt for my first year's salary. Everybody had been trying to lend me money, but I had fought off the most of them on one pretext or another; so this indebtedness represented only £300 borrowed money, the other £300 represented my keep and my purchases. I believed my second year's salary would carry me through the rest of the month if I went on being cautious and economical, and I intended to look sharply out for that. My month ended, my employer back from his journey, I should be all right once more, for I should at once divide the two years' salary among my creditors by assignment, and get right down to my work.

It was a lovely dinner party of fourteen. The Duke and Duchess of Shoreditch, and their daughter the Lady Anne-Grace-Eleanor-Celeste-and-so-forth-and-so-forth-de-Bohun, the Earl and Countess of Newgate, Viscount Cheapside, Lord and Lady Blatherskite, some untitled people of both sexes, the minister and his wife and daughter, and his daughter's visiting friend, an English girl of twenty-two, named Portia Langham, whom I fell in love with in two minutes, and she with me—I could see it without glasses. There was still another guest, an American—but I am a little ahead of my story. While the people were still in the drawing room, whetting up for dinner, and coldly inspecting the late comers, the servant announced:

'Mr. Lloyd Hastings.'

The moment the usual civilities were over, Hastings caught sight of me, and came straight with cordially outstretched hand; then stopped short when about to shake, and said, with an embarrassed look:

'I beg your pardon, sir, I thought I knew you.'

'Why, you do know me, old fellow.'

'No. Are you the—the—'

'Vest-pocket monster? I am, indeed. Don't be afraid to call me by my nickname; I'm used to it.'

'Well, well, well, this is a surprise. Once or twice I've seen your own name coupled with the nickname, but it never occurred to me that you could be the Henry Adams referred to. Why, it isn't six months since you were clerking away for Blake Hopkins in Frisco on a salary, and sitting up nights on an extra allowance, helping me arrange and verify the Gould and Curry Extension papers and statistics. The idea of your being in London, and a vast millionaire, and a colossal celebrity! Why, it's the *Arabian Nights* come again. Man, I can't take it in at all; can't realize it; give me time to settle the whirl in my head.'

'The fact is, Lloyd, you are no worse off than I am. I can't realize it myself.'

'Dear me, it is stunning, now isn't it? Why, it's just three months today since we went to the Miners' restaurant—'

'No; the What Cheer.'

'Right, it was the What Cheer; went there at two in the morning, and had a chop and coffee after a hard six-hours grind over those Extension papers, and I tried to persuade you to come to London with me, and offered to get leave of absence for you and pay all your expenses, and give you something over if I succeeded in making the sale; and you would not listen to me, said I wouldn't succeed, and you couldn't afford to lose the run of business and be no end of time getting the hang of things again when you got back home. And yet here you are. How odd it all is! How did you happen to come, and whatever did give you this incredible start?'

'Oh, just an accident. It's a long story—a romance, a body may say. I'll tell you all about it, but not now.'

'When?'

'The end of this month.'

'That's more than a fortnight yet. It's too much of a strain on a person's curiosity. Make it a week.'

'I can't. You'll know why, by and by. But how's the trade getting along?'

His cheerfulness vanished like a breath, and he said with a sigh:

'You were a true prophet, Hal, a true prophet. I wish I hadn't come. I don't want to talk about it.'

'But you must. You must come and stop with me tonight, when we leave here, and tell me all about it.'

'Oh, may I? Are you in earnest?' and the water showed in his eyes.

'Yes; I want to hear the whole story, every word.'

'I'm so grateful! Just to find a human interest once more, in some voice and in some eye, in me and affairs of mine, after what I've been through here—lord! I could go down on my knees for it!'

He gripped my hand hard, and braced up, and was all right and lively after that for the dinner—which didn't come off. No; the usual thing happened, the thing that is always happening under that vicious and aggravating English system—the matter of precedence couldn't be settled, and so there was no dinner. Englishmen always eat dinner before they go out to dinner, because they know the risks they are running; but nobody ever warns the stranger, and so he walks placidly into trap. Of course, nobody was hurt this time, because we had all been to dinner, none of us being novices excepting Hastings, and he having been informed by the minister at the time that he invited him that in deference to the English custom he had not provided any dinner. Everybody took a lady and processioned down to the dining room, because it is usual to go through the motions; but there the dispute began. The Duke of Shoreditch wanted to take precedence, and sit at the head of the table, holding that he outranked a minister who represented merely a nation and not a monarch; but I stood for my rights, and refused to yield. In the gossip column I ranked all dukes not royal, and said so, and claimed precedence of this one. It couldn't be settled, of course, struggle as we might and did, he finally (and injudiciously) trying to play birth and antiquity, and I 'seeing' his Conqueror and 'raising' him with Adam, whose direct posterity I was, as shown by my name, while he was of a collateral branch, as shown by his, and by his recent Norman origin; so we all processioned back to the drawing room again and had a perpendicular lunch—plate of sardines and a strawberry, and you group yourself and stand up and eat it. Here the religion of precedence is not so strenuous; the two persons of highest rank chuck up a shilling, the one that wins has first go at his strawberry, and the loser gets the shilling. The next two chuck up, then the next two, and so on. After refreshment, tables were brought, and we all played cribbage, sixpence a game. The English never play any game for amusement. If they can't make something or lose something—they don't care which—they won't play.

We had a lovely time; certainly two of us had, Miss Langham and I. I was so bewitched with her that I couldn't count my hands if they went above a double sequence; and when I struck home I never discovered it, and started up the outside row again, and would have lost the game every time, only the girl did the same, she being in just my condition, you see; and consequently neither of us ever got out, or cared to wonder why we didn't; we only just knew we were happy, and didn't wish to know anything else, and didn't want to be interrupted. And I told her—I did, indeed—told her I loved her; and she—well, she blushed till her hair turned red, but she liked it; she said she did. Oh, there was never such an evening! Every time I pegged I put on a postscript; every time she pegged she acknowledged receipt of it, counting the hands the same. Why, I couldn't even say 'Two for his heels' without adding, 'My, how sweet you do look!' and she would say, 'Fifteen two, fifteen four, fifteen six, and a pair are eight, and eight are sixteen—do you think so?'—peeping out aslant from under her lashes, you know, so sweet and cunning. Oh, it was just too-too!

Well, I was perfectly honest and square with her; told her I hadn't a cent in the world but just the million-pound note she'd heard so much talk about, and it didn't belong to me, and that started her curiosity; and then I talked low, and told her the whole history right from the start, and it nearly killed her laughing. What in the nation she could find to laugh about I couldn't see, but there it was; every half-minute some new detail would fetch her, and I would have to stop as much as a minute and a half to give her a chance to settle down again. Why, she laughed herself lame—she did, indeed; I never saw anything like it. I mean I never saw a painful story—a story of a person's troubles and worries and fears—produce just that kind of effect before. So I loved her all the more, seeing she could be so cheerful when there wasn't anything to be cheerful about; for I might soon need that kind of wife, you know, the way things looked. Of course, I told her we should have to wait a couple of years, till I could catch up on my salary; but she didn't mind that, only she hoped I would be as careful as possible in the matter of expenses, and not let them run the least risk of trenching on our third year's pay. Then she began to get a little worried, and wondered if we were making any mistake, and starting the salary on a higher figure for the first year than I would get. This was good sense, and it made me feel a little less confident than I had been feeling before; but it gave me a good business idea, and I brought it frankly out.

'Portia, dear, would you mind going with me that day, when I confront those old gentlemen?'

She shrank a little, but said:

'N-o; if my being with you would help hearten you. But—would it be quite proper, do you think?'

'No, I don't know that it would—in fact, I'm afraid it wouldn't; but, you see, there's so much dependent upon it that—'

'Then I'll go anyway, proper or improper,' she said, with a beautiful and generous enthusiasm. 'Oh, I shall be so happy to think I'm helping!'

'Helping, dear? Why, you'll be doing it all. You're so beautiful and so lovely and so winning, that with you there I can pile our salary up till I break those good old fellows, and they'll never have the heart to struggle.'

Sho! you should have seen the rich blood mount, and her happy eyes shine!

'You wicked flatterer! There isn't a word of truth in what you say, but still I'll go with you. Maybe it will teach you not to expect other people to look with your eyes.'

Were my doubts dissipated? Was my confidence restored? You may judge by this fact: privately I raised my salary to twelve hundred the first year on the spot. But I didn't tell her; I saved it for a surprise.

All the way home I was in the clouds, Hastings talking, I not hearing a word. When he and I entered my parlour, he brought me to myself with his fervent appreciations of my manifold comforts and luxuries.

'Let me just stand here a little and look my fill. Dear me! it's a palace—it's just a palace! And in it everything a body could desire, including cosy coal fire and supper standing ready. Henry, it doesn't merely make me realize how rich you are; it makes me realize, to the bone, to the marrow, how poor I am—how poor I am, and how miserable, how defeated, routed, annihilated!'

Plague take it! this language gave me the cold shudders. It scared me broad awake, and made me comprehend that I was standing on a halfinch crust, with a crater underneath. I didn't know I had been dreaming—that is, I hadn't been allowing myself to know it for a while back; but now—oh, dear! Deep in debt, not a cent in the world, a lovely girl's happiness or woe in my hands, and nothing in front of me but a salary which might never—oh, would never—materialise! Oh, oh, oh! I am ruined past hope! nothing can save me!

'Henry, the mere unconsidered drippings of your daily income would—'

'Oh, my daily income! Here, down with this hot Scotch, and cheer up your soul. Here's with you! Or, no—you're hungry; sit down and—'

'Not a bite for me; I'm past it. I can't eat, these days; but I'll drink with you till I drop. Come!'

'Barrel for barrel, I'm with you! Ready? Here we go! Now, then, Lloyd, unreel your story while I brew.'

'Unreel it? What, again?'

'Again? What do you mean by that?'

'Why, I mean do you want to hear it over again?'

'Do I want to hear it over again? This is a puzzler. Wait; don't take anymore of that liquid. You don't need it.'

'Look here, Henry, you alarm me. Didn't I tell you the whole story on the way here?'

'You?'

'Yes, I.'

'I'll be hanged if I heard a word of it.'

'Henry, this is a serious thing. It troubles me. What did you take up yonder at the minister's?'

Then it all flashed on me, and I owned up like a man.

'I took the dearest girl in this world prisoner!'

So then he came with a rush, and we shook, and shook, and shook till our hands ached; and he didn't blame me for not having heard a word of a story which had lasted while we walked three miles. He just sat down then, like the patient, good fellow he was, and told it all over again. Synopsized, it amounted to this: He had come to England with what he thought was a grand opportunity; he had an 'option' to sell the Gould and Curry Extension for the 'locators' of it, and keep all he could get over a million dollars. He had worked hard, had pulled every wire he knew of, had left no honest expedient untried, had spent nearly all the money he had in the world, had not been able to get a solitary capitalist to listen to him, and his option would run out at the end of the month. In a word, he was ruined. Then he jumped up and cried out:

'Henry, you can save me! You can save me, and you're the only man in the universe that can. Will you do it? Won't you do it?'

'Tell me how. Speak out, my boy.'

'Give me a million and my passage home for my 'option'! Don't, don't refuse!'

I was in a kind of agony. I was right on the point of coming out with the words, 'Lloyd, I'm a pauper myself—absolutely penniless, and in debt!' But a white-hot idea came flaming through my head, and I gripped my jaws together, and calmed myself down till I was as cold as a capitalist. Then I said, in a commercial and self-possessed way:

'I will save you, Lloyd—'

'Then I'm already saved! God be merciful to you forever! If ever I—'

'Let me finish, Lloyd. I will save you, but not in that way; for that would not be fair to you, after your hard work, and the risks you've run. I don't need to buy mines; I can keep my capital moving, in a commercial centre like London, without that; it's what I'm at, all the time; but here is what I'll do. I know all about that mine, of course; I know its immense value, and can swear to it if anybody wishes it. You shall sell out inside of the fortnight for three millions cash, using my name freely, and we'll divide, share and share alike.'

Do you know, he would have danced the furniture to kindling wood in his insane joy, and broken everything on the place, if I hadn't tripped him up and tied him.

Then he lay there, perfectly happy, saying:

'I may use your name! Your name—think of it! Man, they'll flock in droves, these rich Londoners; they'll fight for that stock! I'm a made man, I'm a made man forever, and I'll never forget you as long as I live!'

In less than twenty-four hours London was abuzz! I hadn't anything to do, day after day, but sit at home, and say to all comers:

'Yes; I told him to refer to me. I know the man, and I know the mine. His character is above reproach, and the mine is worth far more than he asks for it.'

Meantime I spent all my evenings at the minister's with Portia. I didn't say a word to her about the mine; I saved it for a surprise. We talked salary; never anything but salary and love; sometimes love, sometimes salary, sometimes love and salary together. And my! the interest the minister's wife and daughter took in our little affair, and the endless ingenuities they invented to save us from interruption, and to keep the minister in the dark and unsuspicious—well, it was just lovely of them!

When the month was up at last, I had a million dollars to my credit in the London and County Bank, and Hastings was fixed in the same way. Dressed at my level best, I drove by the house in Portland Place, judged by the look of things that my birds were home again, went on towards the minister's and got my precious, and we started back, talking salary with all our might. She was so excited and anxious that it made her just intolerably beautiful. I said:

'Dearie, the way you're looking it's a crime to strike for a salary a single penny under three thousand a year.'

'Henry, Henry, you'll ruin us!'

'Don't you be afraid. Just keep up those looks, and trust to me. It'll all come out right.'

So, as it turned out, I had to keep bolstering up her courage all the way. She kept pleading with me, and saying:

'Oh, please remember that if we ask for too much we may get no salary at all; and then what will become of us, with no way in the world to earn our living?'

We were ushered in by that same servant, and there they were, the two old gentlemen. Of course, they were surprised to see that wonderful creature with me, but I said:

'It's all right, gentlemen; she is my future stay and helpmate.'

And I introduced them to her, and called them by name. It didn't surprise them; they knew I would know enough to consult the directory. They seated us, and were very polite to me, and very solicitous to relieve her from embarrassment, and put her as much at her ease as they could. Then I said:

'Gentlemen, I am ready to report.'

'We are glad to hear it,' said my man, 'for now we can decide the bet which my brother Abel and I made. If you have won for me, you shall have any situation in my gift. Have you the million-pound note?'

'Here it is, sir,' and I handed it to him.

'I've won!' he shouted, and slapped Abel on the back. 'Now what do you say, brother?'

'I say he did survive, and I've lost twenty thousand pounds. I never would have believed it.'

'I've a further report to make,' I said, 'and a pretty long one. I want you to let me come soon, and detail my whole month's history; and I promise you it's worth hearing. Meantime, take a look at that.'

'What, man! Certificate of deposit for £200,000. Is it yours?'

'Mine. I earned it by thirty days' judicious use of that little loan you let me have. And the only use I made of it was to buy trifles and offer the bill in change.'

'Come, this is astonishing! It's incredible, man!'

'Never mind, I'll prove it. Don't take my word unsupported.'

But now Portia's turn was come to be surprised. Her eyes were spread wide, and she said:

'Henry, is that really your money? Have you been fibbing to me?'

'I have, indeed, dearie. But you'll forgive me, I know.'

She put up an arch pout, and said:

'Don't you be so sure. You are a naughty thing to deceive me so!'

'Oh, you'll get over it, sweetheart, you'll get over it; it was only fun, you know. Come, let's be going.'

'But wait, wait! The situation, you know. I want to give you the situation,' said my man.

'Well,' I said, 'I'm just as grateful as I can be, but really I don't want one.'

'But you can have the very choicest one in my gift.'

'Thanks again, with all my heart; but I don't even want that one.'

'Henry, I'm ashamed of you. You don't half thank the good gentleman. May I do it for you?'

'Indeed, you shall, dear, if you can improve it. Let us see you try.'

She walked to my man, got up in his lap, put her arm round his neck, and kissed him right on the mouth. Then the two old gentlemen shouted with laughter, but I was dumfounded, just petrified, as you may say. Portia said:

'Papa, he has said you haven't a situation in your gift that he'd take; and I feel just as hurt as—'

'My darling, is that your papa?'

'Yes; he's my step-papa, and the dearest one that ever was. You understand now, don't you, why I was able to laugh when you told me at the minister's, not knowing my relationships, what trouble and worry papa's and Uncle Abel's scheme was giving you?'

Of course, I spoke right up now, without any fooling, and went straight to the point.

'Oh, my dearest dear sir, I want to take back what I said. You have got a situation open that I want.'

'Name it.'

'Son-in-law.'

'Well, well, well! But you know, if you haven't ever served in that capacity, you, of course, can't furnish recommendations of a sort to satisfy the conditions of the contract, and so—'

'Try me—oh, do, I beg of you! Only just try me thirty or forty years, and if—'

'Oh, well, all right; it's but a little thing to ask, take her along.'

Happy, we two? There are not words enough in the unabridged to describe it. And when London got the whole history, a day or two later, of my month's adventures with that bank-note, and how they ended, did London talk, and have a good time? Yes.

My Portia's papa took that friendly and hospitable bill back to the Bank of England and cashed it; then the Bank cancelled it and made him a present of it, and he gave it to us at our wedding, and it has always hung in its frame in the sacredest place in our home ever since. For it gave me my Portia. But for it I could not have remained in London, would not have appeared at the minister's, never should have met her. And so I always say, 'Yes, it's a million-pounder, as you see; but it never made but one purchase in its life, and then got the article for only about a tenth part of its value.'

About the Author

Samuel Langhorne Clemens (November 30, 1835 - April 21, 1910), better known by his pen name Mark Twain, was an American author and humourist. He is most noted for his novel *The Adventures of Tom Sawyer* (1876) and its sequel, *Adventures of Huckleberry Finn* (1885).

The Canterville Ghost

Oscar Wilde

When Mr. Hiram B. Otis, the American Minister, bought Canterville Chase, everyone told him he was doing a very foolish thing, as there was no doubt at all that the place was haunted. Indeed, Lord Canterville himself, who was a man of the most punctilious honour, had felt it his duty to mention the fact to Mr. Otis when they came to discuss terms.

'We have not cared to live in the place ourselves,' said Lord Canterville, 'since my grand-aunt, the Dowager Duchess of Bolton, was frightened into a fit, from which she never really recovered, by two skeleton hands being placed on her shoulders as she was dressing for dinner, and I feel bound to tell you, Mr. Otis, that the ghost has been seen by several living members of my family, as well as by the rector of the parish, the Rev. Augustus Dampier, who is a Fellow of King's College, Cambridge. After the unfortunate accident to the Duchess, none of our younger servants would stay with us, and Lady

Canterville often got very little sleep at night, in consequence of the mysterious noises that came from the corridor and the library.'

A few weeks later though, the purchase was concluded, and at the close of the season the Minister and his family went down to Canterville Chase. Mrs. Otis, who, as Miss Lucretia R. Tappan, of West 53rd Street, had been a celebrated New York belle, was now a very handsome, middle-aged woman, with fine eyes, and a superb profile. Their eldest son, christened Washington by his parents in a moment of patriotism, which he never ceased to regret, was a fair-haired, rather good-looking young man, who had qualified himself for American diplomacy by leading the German at the Newport Casino for three successive seasons, and even in London was well known as an excellent dancer. Miss Virginia E. Otis was a little girl of fifteen, lithe and lovely as a fawn, and with a fine freedom in her large blue eyes. After Virginia came the twins, who were usually called 'The Stars and Stripes,' as they were always getting swished. They were delightful boys.

As Canterville Chase is seven miles from Ascot, the nearest railway station, Mr. Otis had telegraphed for a waggonette to meet them, and they started on their drive in high spirits. It was a lovely July evening, and the air was delicate with the scent of the pinewoods. As they entered the avenue of Canterville Chase, however, the sky became suddenly overcast with clouds, a curious stillness seemed to hold the atmosphere, a great flight of rooks passed silently over their heads, and, before they reached the house, some big drops of rain had fallen.

Standing on the steps to receive them was an old woman, neatly dressed in black silk, with a white cap and apron. This was Mrs. Umney, the housekeeper, whom Mrs. Otis, at Lady Canterville's earnest request, had consented to keep on in her former position. She made them each a low curtsey as they alighted, and said in a quaint, old-fashioned manner, 'I bid you welcome to Canterville Chase.' Following her, they passed through the fine Tudor hall into the library, a long, low room, panelled in black oak, at the end of which was a large stained-glass window. Here they found tea laid out for them, and, after taking off their wraps, they sat down and began to look round, while Mrs. Umney waited on them.

Suddenly Mrs. Otis caught sight of a dull red stain on the floor just by the fireplace and, quite unconscious of what it really signified, said to Mrs. Umney, 'I am afraid something has been spilt there.'

'Yes, madam,' replied the old housekeeper in a low voice, 'blood has been spilt on that spot.'

'How horrid,' cried Mrs. Otis; 'I don't at all care for bloodstains in a sitting room. It must be removed at once.'

The old woman smiled, and answered in the

same low, mysterious voice, 'It is the blood of Lady Eleanore de Canterville, who was murdered on that very spot by her own husband, Sir Simon de Canterville, in 1575. Sir Simon survived her nine years, and disappeared suddenly under very mysterious circumstances. His body has never been discovered, but his guilty spirit still haunts the Chase. The bloodstain has been much admired by tourists and others, and cannot be removed.'

'That is all nonsense,' cried Washington Otis; 'Pinkerton's Champion Stain Remover and Paragon Detergent will clean it up in no time,' and before the terrified housekeeper could interfere he had fallen upon his knees, and was rapidly scouring the floor with a small stick of what looked like a black cosmetic. In a few moments no trace of the bloodstain could be seen.

'I knew Pinkerton would do it,' he exclaimed triumphantly, as he looked round at his admiring family; but no sooner had he said these words than a terrible flash of lightning lit up the sombre room, a fearful peal of thunder made them all start to their feet, and Mrs. Umney fainted.

'What a monstrous climate!' said the American Minister calmly, as he lit a long cheroot. 'I guess the old country is so over-populated that they have not enough decent weather for everybody. I have always been of opinion that emigration is the only thing for England.

'My dear Hiram,' cried Mrs. Otis, 'what can we do with a woman who faints?'

'Charge it to her like breakages,' answered the Minister; 'she won't faint after that;' and in a few moments Mrs. Umney certainly came to. There was no doubt, however, that she was extremely upset, and she sternly warned Mr. Otis to beware of some trouble coming to the house.

'I have seen things with my own eyes, sir,' she said,'that would make any Christian's hair stand on end, and many and many a night I have not closed my eyes in sleep for the awful things that are done here.' Mr. Otis, however, and his wife warmly assured the honest soul that they were not afraid of ghosts, and, after invoking the blessings of Providence on her new master and mistress, and making arrangements for an increase of salary, the old housekeeper tottered off to her own room.

The storm raged fiercely all that night, but nothing of particular note occurred. The next morning, however, when they came down to breakfast, they found the terrible stain of blood once again on the floor. 'I don't think it can be the fault of the Paragon Detergent,' said Washington,' for I have tried it with everything. It must be the ghost.' He accordingly rubbed out the stain a second time, but the second morning it appeared again. The third morning also it was there, though the library had been locked up at night by Mr. Otis himself, and the key carried upstairs. The whole family were now quite interested; Mr. Otis began to suspect that he had been too dogmatic in his denial of the existence of ghosts, Mrs. Otis expressed her intention of joining the Psychical Society, and Washington prepared a long letter to Messrs. Myers and Podmore on the subject of the Permanence of Sanguineous Stains when connected with Crime. That night all doubts about the objective existence of phantasmata were removed for ever.

The day had been warm and sunny; and, in the cool of the evening, the whole family went out to drive. They did not return home till nine o'clock, when they had a light supper. No mention at all was made of the supernatural, nor was Sir Simon de Canterville alluded to in any way. At eleven o'clock the family retired, and by half-past all the lights were out. Some time after, Mr. Otis was awakened by a curious noise in the corridor, outside his room. It sounded like the clank of metal, and seemed to be coming nearer every moment. He got up at once, struck a match, and looked at the time. It was exactly one o'clock. He was quite calm, and felt his pulse, which was not at all feverish. The strange noise still continued, and with it he heard distinctly the sound of footsteps. He put on his slippers, took a small oblong phial out of his dressing case, and opened the door. Right in front of him he saw, in the wan moonlight, an old man of terrible aspect. His eyes were as red burning coals; long grey hair fell over his shoulders in matted coils; his garments, which were of antique cut, were soiled and ragged, and from his wrists and ankles hung heavy manacles and rusty gyves.

'My dear sir,' said Mr. Otis,'I really must insist on your oiling those chains, and have brought you for that purpose a small bottle of the Tammany Rising Sun Lubricator. It is said to be completely efficacious upon one application, and there are several testimonials to that effect on the wrapper from some of our most eminent native divines. I shall leave it here for you by the bedroom candles, and will be happy to supply you with more should you require it.' With these words the United States Minister laid the bottle down on a marble table, and, closing his door, retired to rest.

For a moment the Canterville ghost stood quite motionless in natural indignation; then, dashing the bottle violently upon the polished floor, he fled down the corridor, uttering hollow groans, and emitting a ghastly green light. Just, however, as he reached the top of the great oak staircase, a door was flung open, two little white-robed figures appeared, and a large pillow whizzed past his head! There was evidently no time to be lost, so, hastily adopting the Fourth Dimension of Space as a means of escape, he vanished through the wainscoting, and the house became quite quiet.

On reaching a small secret chamber in the left wing, he leaned up against a moonbeam to recover his breath, and began to try and realize his position.

Never, in a brilliant and uninterrupted career of three hundred years, had he been so grossly insulted. It was quite unbearable. Besides, no ghost in history had ever been treated in this manner. Accordingly, he determined to have vengeance, and remained till daylight in an attitude of deep thought.

The next morning, when the Otis family met at breakfast, they discussed the ghost at some length. The United States Minister was naturally a little annoyed to find that his present had not been accepted. 'I have no wish,' he said, 'to do the ghost any personal injury, and I must say that considering the length of time he has been in the house, I don't think it is at all polite to throw pillows at him. If he really declines to use the Rising Sun Lubricator, we shall have to take his chains from him. It would be quite impossible to sleep, with such a noise going on outside the bedrooms.'

For the rest of the week, however, they were undisturbed, the only thing that excited any attention being the continual renewal of the bloodstain on the library floor. This certainly was very strange, as the door was always locked at night by Mr. Otis, and the windows kept closely barred. The chameleon-like colour, also, of the stain excited a good deal of comment. Some mornings it was a dull (almost Indian) red, then it would be vermilion, then a rich purple, and once when they came down for family prayers, according to the simple rites of the Free American Reformed Episcopalian Church, they found it a bright emerald green. These kaleidoscopic changes naturally amused the party very much, and bets on the subject were freely made every evening. The only person who did not enter into the joke was little Virginia, who, for some unexplained reason, was always a good deal distressed at the sight of the bloodstain, and very nearly cried the morning it was emerald green.

The second appearance of the ghost was on Sunday night. Shortly after they had gone to bed they were suddenly alarmed by a fearful crash in the hall. Rushing downstairs, they found that a large suit of old armour had become detached from its stand, and had fallen on the stone floor, while, seated in a highbacked chair, was the Canterville ghost, rubbing his knees with an expression of acute agony on his face. The twins, having brought their pea-shooters with them, at once discharged two pellets on him, with that accuracy of aim which can only be attained by long and careful practice on a writing-master, while the United States Minister covered him with his revolver, and called upon him, in accordance with Californian etiquette, to hold up his hands! The ghost started up with a wild shriek of rage, and swept through them like a mist, extinguishing Washington

Otis's candle as he passed, and so leaving them all in total darkness. On reaching the top of the staircase he recovered himself, and determined to give his celebrated peal of demoniac laughter. This he had on more than one occasion found extremely useful. It was said to have turned Lord Raker's wig grey in a single night, and had certainly made three of Lady Canterville's French governesses give warning before their month was up. He accordingly laughed his most horrible laugh, till the old vaulted roof rang and rang again, but hardly had the fearful echo died away when a door opened, and Mrs. Otis came out in a light blue dressing gown. 'I am afraid you are far from well,' she said, 'and have brought you a bottle of Dr. Dobell's tincture. If it is indigestion, you will find it a most excellent remedy.' The ghost glared at her in fury, and began at once to make preparations for turning himself into a large black dog, an accomplishment for which he was justly renowned, and to which the family doctor always attributed the permanent idiocy of Lord Canterville's uncle, the Hon. Thomas Horton. The sound of approaching footsteps, however, made him hesitate in his fell purpose, so he contented himself with becoming faintly phosphorescent, and vanished with a deep churchyard groan, just as the twins had come up to him.

On reaching his room he entirely broke down, and became a prey to the most violent agitation. The vulgarity of the twins, and the gross materialism of Mrs. Otis, were naturally extremely annoying, but what really distressed him most was that he had been unable to wear the suit of mail. He had hoped that even modern Americans would be thrilled by the sight of a spectre in armour, if for no more sensible reason, at least out of respect for their national poet Longfellow, over whose graceful and attractive poetry he himself had whiled away many a weary hour when the Cantervilles were up in town. Besides, it was his own suit. He had worn it with great success at the Kenilworth tournament, and had been highly complimented on it by no less a person than the Virgin Queen herself. Yet when he had put it on, he had been completely overpowered by the weight of the huge breastplate and steel casque, and had fallen heavily on the stone pavement, barking both his knees severely, and bruising the knuckles of his right hand.

For some days after this he was extremely ill, and hardly stirred out of his room at all, except to keep the bloodstain in proper repair. However, by taking great care of himself, he recovered, and resolved to make a third attempt to frighten the United States Minister and his family. He selected Friday, the 17th of August, for his appearance, and spent most of that day in looking over his wardrobe, ultimately deciding in favour of a large slouched hat with a red feather, a windingsheet frilled at the wrists and neck, and a rusty dagger. Towards evening a violent storm of rain came on, and the wind was so high that all the windows and doors in the old house shook and rattled. In fact, it was just such weather as he loved. His plan of action was this. He was to make his way quietly to Washington Otis's room, gibber at him from the foot of the bed, and stab himself three times in the throat to the sound of slow music. He bore Washington a special grudge, being quite aware that it was he who was in the habit of removing the famous Canterville bloodstain, by means of Pinkerton's Paragon Detergent. Having reduced the reckless and foolhardy youth to a condition of abject terror, he was then to proceed to the room occupied by the United States Minister and his wife, and there to place a clammy hand on Mrs. Otis's forehead, while he hissed into her trembling husband's ear the awful secrets of the charnel house. With regard to little Virginia, he had not quite made up his mind. She had never insulted him in any way, and was pretty and gentle. A few hollow groans from the wardrobe, he thought, would be more than sufficient, or, if that failed to wake her, he might grabble at the counterpane with palsy-twitching fingers. As for the twins, he was quite determined to teach them a lesson. The first thing to be done was, of course, to sit upon their chests, so as to produce the stifling sensation of nightmare. Then, as their beds were quite close to each other, to stand between them in the form of a green, icy-cold corpse, till they became paralysed with fear, and finally, to throw off the winding sheet, and crawl round the room, with white, bleached bones and one rolling eyeball, in the character of 'Dumb Daniel, or the Suicide's Skeleton,' a role in which he had on more than one occasion produced a great effect, and which he considered quite equal to his famous part of 'Martin the Maniac, or the Masked Mystery.'

At half-past ten he heard the family going to bed. For some time he was disturbed by wild shrieks of laughter from the twins, who, with the light-hearted gaiety of schoolboys, were evidently amusing themselves before they retired to rest, but at a quarterpast eleven all was still, and, as midnight sounded, he sallied forth. The owl beat against the window panes, the raven croaked from the old yew tree, and the wind wandered moaning round the house like a lost soul; but the Otis family slept unconscious of their doom, and high above the rain and storm he could hear the steady snoring of the Minister for the United States. He stepped stealthily out of the wainscoting, with an evil smile on his cruel, wrinkled mouth, and the moon hid her face in a cloud as he stole past the great oriel window, where his own arms and those of his murdered wife were blazoned in azure and gold. On and on he glided, like an evil shadow, the very darkness seeming to loathe him as he passed. Once he thought he heard something call, and stopped; but it was only the baying of a dog from the Red Farm, and he went on, muttering strange sixteenth-century curses, and ever and anon brandishing the rusty dagger in the midnight air. Finally he reached the corner of the passage that led to luckless Washington's room. For a moment he paused there, the wind blowing his long grey locks about his head, and twisting into grotesque and fantastic folds the nameless horror of the dead man's shroud. Then the clock struck the quarter, and he felt the time was come. He chuckled to himself, and turned the corner; but no sooner had he done so, than, with a piteous wail of terror, he fell back, and hid his blanched face in his long, bony hands. Right in front of him was standing a horrible spectre, motionless as a carven image, and monstrous as a madman's dream! Its head was bald and burnished; its face round, and fat, and white; and hideous laughter seemed to have writhed its features into an eternal grin. From the eyes streamed rays of scarlet light, the mouth was a wide well of fire, and a hideous garment, like to his own, swathed with its silent snows the Titan form. On its breast was a placard with strange writing in antique characters, some scroll of shame it seemed, some record of wild sins, some awful calendar of crime, and, with its right hand, it bore aloft a falchion of gleaming steel.

Never having seen a ghost before, he naturally

was terribly frightened, and, after a second hasty glance at the awful phantom, he fled back to his room, tripping up in his long winding sheet as he sped down the corridor, and finally dropping the rusty dagger into the Minister's jack boots, where it was found in the morning by the butler. Once in the privacy of his own apartment, he flung himself down on a small pallet-bed, and hid his face under the clothes. After a time, however, the brave old Canterville spirit asserted itself, and he determined to go and speak to the other ghost as soon as it was daylight. Accordingly, just as the dawn was touching the hills with silver, he returned towards the spot where he had first laid eyes on the grisly phantom, feeling that, after all, two ghosts were better than one, and that, by the aid of his new friend, he might safely grapple with the twins. On reaching the spot, however, a terrible sight met his gaze. Something had evidently happened to the spectre, for the light had entirely faded from its hollow eyes, the gleaming falchion had fallen from its hand, and it was leaning up against the wall in a strained and uncomfortable attitude. He rushed forward and seized it in his arms, when, to his horror, the head slipped off and rolled on the floor, the body assumed a recumbent posture, and he found himself clasping a white dimity bed-curtain, with a sweeping-brush, a kitchen cleaver, and a hollow turnip lying at his feet! Unable to understand this curious transformation, he clutched the placard with feverish haste, and there, in the grey morning light, he read these fearful words:—

YE OTIS GHOSTE.
Ye Onlie true and Originale Spook.
Beware of Ye Imitationes.
All others are Counterfeite.

The whole thing flashed across him. He had been tricked, foiled, and outwitted! The old Canterville look came into his eyes; he ground his toothless gums together; and, raising his withered hands high above his head, swore, according to the picturesque phraseology of the antique school, that when Chanticleer had sounded twice his merry horn, deeds of blood would be wrought, and Murder walk abroad with silent feet.

Hardly had he finished this awful oath when, from the red-tiled roof of a distant homestead, a cock crew. He laughed a long, low, bitter laugh, and waited. Hour after hour he waited, but the cock, for some strange reason, did not crow again. Finally, at half-past seven, the arrival of the housemaids made him give up his fearful vigil, and he stalked back to his room, thinking of his vain oath and baffled purpose. There he consulted several books of ancient chivalry, of which he was exceedingly fond, and found that, on every occasion on which his oath had been used, Chanticleer had always crowed a second time. 'Perdition seize the naughty fowl,' he muttered, 'I have seen the day when, with my stout spear, I would have run him through the gorge, and made him crow for me an 'twere in death!' He then retired to a comfortable lead coffin, and stayed there till evening.

The next day the ghost was very weak and tired. The terrible excitement of the last four weeks was beginning to have its effect. His nerves were completely shattered, and he started at the slightest noise. For five days he kept his room, and at last made up his mind to give up the point of the bloodstain on the library floor. If the Otis family did not want it, they clearly did not deserve it. They were evidently people on a low, material plane of existence, and quite incapable of appreciating the symbolic value of sensuous phenomena. The question of phantasmic apparitions, and the development of astral bodies, was, of course, quite a different matter, and really not under his control. It was his solemn duty to appear in the corridor once a week, and to gibber from the large oriel window on the first and third Wednesdays in every month, and he did not see how he could honourably escape from his obligations. It is quite true that his life had been very evil, but, upon the other hand, he was most conscientious in all things connected with the supernatural. For the next three Saturdays, accordingly, he traversed the corridor as usual between midnight and three o'clock, taking every possible precaution against being either heard or seen. He removed his boots, trod as lightly as possible on the old worm-eaten boards, wore a large black velvet cloak, and was careful to use the Rising Sun Lubricator for oiling his chains. I am bound to acknowledge that it was with a good deal of difficulty that he brought himself to adopt this last mode of protection. However, one night, while the family were at dinner, he slipped into Mr. Otis's bedroom and carried off the bottle. He felt a little humiliated at first, but afterwards was sensible enough to see that there was a great deal to be said for the invention, and, to a certain degree, it served his purpose. Still, in spite of everything, he was not left unmolested. Strings were continually being stretched across the corridor, over which he tripped in the dark, and on one occasion, while dressed for the part of 'Black Isaac, or the Huntsman of Hogley Woods', he met with a severe fall, through treading on a butter slide, which the twins had constructed from the entrance of the Tapestry Chamber to the top of the oak staircase. This last insult so enraged him that he resolved to make one final effort to assert his dignity and social position, and determined to visit the insolent young Etonians the next night in his celebrated character of 'Reckless Rupert, or the Headless Earl'.

He had not appeared in this disguise for more than seventy years; in fact, not since he had so frightened pretty Lady Barbara Modish by means of it, that she suddenly broke off her engagement with the present Lord Canterville's grandfather, and ran away to Gretna Green with handsome Jack Castleton, declaring that nothing in the world would induce her to marry into a family that allowed such a horrible phantom to walk up and down the terrace at twilight. Poor Jack was afterwards shot in a duel by Lord Canterville on Wandsworth Common, and Lady Barbara died of a broken heart at Tunbridge Wells before the year was out, so, in every way, it had been a great success. It was, however, an extremely dimcult 'make-up', if I may use such a theatrical expression in connection with one of the greatest mysteries of the supernatural, or, to employ a more scientific term, the higher natural world, and it took him fully three hours to make his preparations. At last everything was ready, and he was very pleased with his appearance. The big leather riding boots that went with the dress were just a little too large for him, and he could only find one of the two horse pistols, but, on the whole, he was quite satisfied, and at a quarter past one he glided out of the wainscoting and crept down the corridor. On reaching the room occupied by the twins, which I should mention was called the Blue Bed Chamber, on account of the colour of its hangings, he found the door just ajar. Wishing to make an effective entrance, he flung it wide open, when a heavy jug of water fell right down on him, wetting him to the skin, and just missing his left shoulder by a couple of inches. At the same moment he heard stifled shrieks of laughter proceeding from the four-post bed. The shock to his nervous system was so great that he fled back to his room as hard as he could go, and the next day he was laid up with a severe cold. The only thing that at all consoled him in the whole affair was the fact that he had not brought his head with him, for, had he done so, the consequences might have been very serious.

He now gave up all hope of ever frightening this rude American family, and contented himself, as a rule, with creeping about the passages in list slippers, with a thick red muffler round his throat for fear of draughts, and a small arquebuse, in case he should be attacked by the twins. The final blow he received occurred on the 19th of September. He had gone downstairs to the great entrance hall, feeling sure that there, at any rate, he would be quite unmolested, and was amusing himself by making satirical remarks on the large Saroni photographs of the United States Minister and his wife, which had now taken the place of the Canterville family pictures. He was simply but neatly clad in a long shroud, spotted with churchyard mould, had tied up his jaw with a strip of yellow linen, and carried a small lantern and a sexton's spade. In fact, he was dressed for the character of 'Jonas the Graveless, or the Corpse-Snatcher of Chertsey Barn,' one of his most remarkable impersonations, and one which the Cantervilles had every reason to remember, as it was the real origin of their quarrel with their neighbour, Lord Rufford. It was about a quarter past two o'clock in the morning, and, as far as he could ascertain, no one was stirring. As he was stroilling towards the library, however, to see if there were any traces left of the bloodstain, suddenly there leaped out on him from a dark corner two figures, who waved their arms wildly above their heads, and shrieked out 'BOO!' in his ear.

Seized with a panic, which, under the circumstances, was only natural, he rushed for the staircase, but found Washington Otis waiting for him there with the big garden syringe; and being thus hemmed in by his enemies on every side, and driven almost to bay, he vanished into the great iron stove, which, fortunately for him, was not lit, and had to make his way home through the flues and chimneys, arriving at his own room in a terrible state of dirt, disorder and despair.

After this he was not seen again on any nocturnal expedition. The twins lay in wait for him on several occasions, and strewed the passages with nutshells every night to the great annoyance of their parents and the servants, but it was of no avail. It was quite evident that his feelings were so wounded that he would not appear. Mr. Otis consequently resumed his great work on the history of the Democratic

Party, on which he had been engaged for some years; Mrs. Otis organised a wonderful clam bake, which amazed the whole county; the boys took to lacrosse, euchre, poker, and other American national games; and Virginia rode about the lanes on her pony, accompanied by the young Duke of Cheshire, who had come to spend the last week of his holidays at Canterville Chase. It was generally assumed that the ghost had gone away, and, in fact, Mr. Otis wrote a letter to that effect to Lord Canterville, who, in reply, expressed his great pleasure at the news, and sent his best congratulations to the Minister's worthy wife.

The Otises, however, were deceived, for the ghost was still in the house, and though now almost an invalid, was by no means ready to let matters rest, particularly as he heard that among the guests was the young Duke of Cheshire, whose grand-uncle, Lord Francis Stilton, had once bet a hundred guineas with Colonel Carbury that he would play dice with the Canterville ghost, and was found the next morning lying on the floor of the card room in such a helpless paralytic state that though he lived on to a great age, he was never able to say anything again but 'Double Sixes.' The story was well known at the time, though, of course, out of respect to the feelings of the two noble families, every attempt was made to hush it up; and a full account of all the circumstances connected with it will be found in the third volume of Lord Tattle's 'Recollections of the Prince Regent and his Friends'. The ghost, then, was naturally very anxious to show that he had not lost his influence over the Stiltons, with whom, indeed, he was distantly connected, his own first cousin having been married en secondes noces, the Sieur de Bulkeley, from whom, as everyone knows, the Dukes of Cheshire are lineally descended. Accordingly, he made arrangements for appearing to Virginia's little lover in his celebrated impersonation of 'The Vampire Monk, or, the Bloodless Benedictine,' a performance so horrible that when old Lady Startup saw it, which she did on one fatal New Year's Eve, in the year 1764, she went off into the most piercing shrieks, which culminated in violent apoplexy, and died in three days, after disinheriting the Cantervilles, who were her nearest relations, and leaving all her money to her London apothecary. At the last moment, however, his terror of the twins prevented his leaving his room, and the little Duke slept in peace under the great feathered canopy in the Royal Bedchamber, and dreamed of Virginia.

A few days after this, Virginia and her curly-haired cavalier went out riding on Brockley meadows, where she tore her habit so badly in getting through a hedge, that, on their return home, she made up her mind to go up by the back staircase so as not to be seen. As she was running past the Tapestry Chamber, the door of which happened to be open, she fancied she saw someone inside, and thinking it was her mother's maid, who sometimes used to bring her work there, looked in to ask her to mend her habit. To her immense surprise, however, it was the Canterville Ghost himself! He was sitting by the window, watching the ruined gold of the yellowing trees fly through the air, and the red leaves dancing madly down the long avenue. His head was leaning on his hand, and his whole attitude was one of extreme depression. Indeed, so forlorn, and so much out of repair did he look, that little Virginia, whose first idea had been to run away and lock herself in her room, was filled with pity, and determined to try and comfort him. So light was her footfall, and so deep his melancholy, that he was not aware of her presence till she spoke to him.

'I am so sorry for you,' she said, 'but my brothers are going back to Eton tomorrow, and then, if you behave yourself, no one will annoy you.'

'It is absurd asking me to behave myself,' he answered, looking round in astonishment at the pretty little girl who had ventured to address him, quite absurd. 'I must rattle my chains, and groan through keyholes, and walk about at night, if that is what you mean. It is my only reason for existing.'

'It is no reason at all for existing, and you know you have been very wicked. Mrs. Umney told us, the first day we arrived here, that you had killed your wife.'

'Well, I quite admit it,' said the Ghost petulantly, 'but it was a purely family matter, and concerned no one else.'

'It is very wrong to kill anyone,' said Virginia, who at times had a sweet Puritan gravity, caught from some old New England ancestor.

'Oh, I hate the cheap severity of abstract ethics! My wife was very plain, never had my ruffs properly starched, and knew nothing about cookery. Why, there was a buck I had shot in Hogley Woods, a magnificent pricket, and do you know how she had it sent up to table? However, it is no matter now, for it is all over, and I don't think it was very nice of her brothers to starve me to death, though I did kill her.'

'Starve you to death? Oh, Mr. Ghost, I mean Sir Simon, are you hungry? I have a sandwich in my case. Would you like it?'

'No, thank you, I never eat anything now; but it is very kind of you, all the same, and you are much nicer than the rest of your horrid, rude, vulgar, dishonest family.'

'Stop!' cried Virginia, stamping her foot, 'it is you who are rude, and horrid, and vulgar, and as for dishonesty, you know you stole the paints out of my box to try and furbish up that ridiculous bloodstain in the library. First you took all my reds, including the vermilion, and I couldn't do any more sunsets, then you took the emerald green and the chrome yellow, and finally I had nothing left but indigo and Chinese white, and could only do moonlight scenes, which are always depressing to look at, and not at all easy to paint. I never told on you, though I was very much annoyed, and it was most ridiculous, the whole thing; for who ever heard of emerald-green blood?'

'Well, really,' said the Ghost, rather meekly, 'what was I to do? It is a very difficult thing to get real blood nowadays, and, as your brother began it all with his Paragon Detergent, I certainly saw no reason why I should not have your paints. As for colour, that is always a matter of taste: the Cantervilles have blue blood, for instance, the very bluest in England; but I know you Americans don't care for things of this kind.'

'You know nothing about it, and the best thing you can do is to emigrate and improve your mind. My father will be only too happy to give you a free passage, and though there is a heavy duty on spirits of every kind, there will be no difficulty about the Custom House, as the officers are all Democrats. Once in New York, you are sure to be a great success. I know lots of people there who would give a hundred thousand dollars to have a grandfather and much more than that to have a family ghost.'

'I don't think I should like America.'

'I suppose because we have no ruins and no curiosities,' said Virginia satirically.

'No ruins! no curiosities!' answered the Ghost, 'you have your navy and your manners.'

'Good evening; I will go and ask papa to get the twins an extra week's holiday.'

'Please don't go, Miss Virginia,' he cried; I am so lonely and so unhappy, and I really don't know what to do. I want to go to sleep and I cannot.'

'That's quite absurd! You have merely to go to bed and blow out the candle. It is very difficult sometimes to keep awake, especially at church, but there is no difficulty at all about sleeping. Why, even babies know how to do that, and they are not very clever.'

'I have not slept for three hundred years,' he said sadly, and Virginia's beautiful blue eyes opened in wonder; 'for three hundred years I have not slept, and I am so tired.'

Virginia grew quite grave, and her little lips trembled like rose leaves. She came towards him, and kneeling down at his side, looked up into his old withered face.

'Poor, poor Ghost,' she murmured, 'have you no place where you can sleep?'

'Far away beyond the pine woods,' he answered, in a low dreamy voice, 'there is a little garden. There the grass grows long and deep, there are the great white stars of the hemlock flower, there the nightingale sings all night long. All night long he sings, and the cold, crystal moon looks down, and the yew tree spreads out its giant arms over the sleepers.'

Virginia's eyes grew dim with tears, and she hid her face in her hands.

'You mean the Garden of Death,' she whispered.

'Yes, Death. Death must be so beautiful. To lie in the soft brown earth, with the grasses waving above one's head, and listen to silence. To have no yesterday, and no tomorrow. To forget time, to forgive life, to be at peace. You can help me. You can open for me the portals of Death's house, for Love is always with you, and Love is stronger than Death is.'

Virginia trembled, a cold shudder ran through her, and for a few moments there was silence. She felt as if she was in a terrible dream.

Then the Ghost spoke again, and his voice sounded like the sighing of the wind.

'Have you ever read the old prophecy on the library window?'

'Oh, often,' cried the little girl, looking up; 'I know it quite well. It is painted in curious black letters, and it is difficult to read. There are only six lines:

Whan a golden girl can win
Prayer from out the lips of sin,
When the barren almond bears,
And a little child give away its tears,
Then shall all the house be still
And peace come to Canterville.

But I don't know what they mean.'

'They mean,' he said sadly, 'that you must weep with me for my sins, because I have no tears, and pray with me for my soul, because I have no faith, and then, if you have always been sweet, and good, and gentle, the Angel of Death will have mercy on me. You will see fearful shapes in darkness, and wicked voices will whisper in your ear, but they will not harm you, for against the purity of a little child the powers of Hell cannot prevail.'

Virginia made no answer, and the Ghost wrung his hands in wild despair as he looked down at her bowed golden head. Suddenly she stood up, very pale, and with a strange light in her eyes. 'I am not afraid,' she said firmly, 'and I will ask the Angel to have mercy on you.'

He rose from his seat with a faint cry of joy, and taking her hand bent over it with old-fashioned grace and kissed it. His fingers were as cold as ice, and his lips burned like fire, but Virginia did not falter, as he led her across the dusky room. On the faded green tapestry were broidered little huntsmen. They blew their tasselled horns and with their tiny hands waved to her to go back. 'Go back! little Virginia,' they cried, 'go back!' but the Ghost clutched her hand more tightly, and she shut her eyes against them. Horrible animals with lizard tails, and goggle eyes, blinked at her from the carven chimney piece, and murmured 'Beware! little Virginia, beware! we may never see you again,' but the Ghost glided on more swiftly, and Virginia did not listen.

When they reached the end of the room, he stopped, and muttered some words she could not understand. She opened her eyes, and saw the wall slowly fading away like a mist, and a great black cavern in front of her. A bitter cold wind swept round them, and she felt something pulling at her dress. 'Quick, quick,' cried the Ghost, 'or it will be too late,' and, in a moment, the wainscoting had closed behind them, and the Tapestry Chamber was empty.

About ten minutes later, the bell rang for tea, and, as Virginia did not come down, Mrs. Otis sent up one of the footmen to tell her. After a little time he returned and said that he could not find Miss Virginia anywhere. As she was in the habit of going out to the garden every evening to get flowers for the dinner table, Mrs. Otis was not at all alarmed at first, but when six o'clock struck, and Virginia did not appear, she became really agitated, and sent the boys out to look for her, while she herself and Mr. Otis searched every room in the house. At half past six the boys came back and said that they could find no trace of their sister anywhere. They were all now in the greatest state of excitement, and did not know what to do, when Mr. Otis suddenly remembered that, some few days before, he had given a band of gipsies permission to camp in the park. He accordingly at once set off for Blackfell Hollow, where he knew they were, accompanied by his eldest son and two of the farm servants. The little Duke of Cheshire, who was perfectly frantic with anxiety, begged hard to be allowed to go too, but Mr. Otis would not allow him, as he was afraid there might be a scuffle. On arriving at the spot, however, he found that the gipsies had gone, and it was evident that their departure had been rather sudden, as the fire was still burning, and some plates were lying on the grass. Having sent off Washington and the two men to scour the district, he ran home, and despatched telegrams to all the police inspectors in the county, telling them to look out for a little girl who had been kidnapped by tramps or gipsies. He then ordered his horse to be brought round, and, after insisting on his wife and the three boys sitting down to dinner, rode off down the Ascot road with a groom. He had hardly, however, gone a couple of miles, when he heard somebody galloping after him, and, looking round, saw the little Duke coming up on his pony, with his face very flushed and no hat. 'I'm awfully sorry, Mr. Otis,' gasped out the boy, 'but I can't eat any dinner as long as Virginia is lost. Please, don't be angry with me; if you had let us be engaged last year, there would never have been all this trouble. You won't send me back, will you? I can't go! I won't go!'

The Minister could not help smiling at the handsome young scapegrace, and was a good deal touched at his devotion to Virginia, so leaning down from his horse, he patted him kindly on the shoulders, and said, 'Well, Cecil, if you won't go back I suppose you must come with me, but I must get you a hat at Ascot.'

'Oh, bother my hat! I want Virginia!' cried the little Duke, laughing, and they galloped on to the railway station. There Mr. Otis inquired of the station master if anyone answering to the description of Virginia had been seen on the platform, but could get no news of her. The station master, however, wired up and down the line, and assured him that a strict watch would be kept for her, and, after having bought a hat for the little Duke from a linen draper, who was just putting up his shutters, Mr. Otis rode off to Bexley, a village about four miles away, which he was told was a well-known haunt of the gipsies, as there was a large common next to it. Here they roused up the rural policeman, but could get no information from him, and, after riding all over the common, they turned their horses' heads homewards, and reached the Chase about eleven o'clock, dead tired and almost heartbroken. They found Washington and the twins waiting for them at the gate house with lanterns, as the avenue was very dark. Not the slightest trace of Virginia had been discovered. The gipsies had been caught on Brockley meadows, but she was not with them, and they had explained their sudden departure by saying that they had mistaken the date of Chorton Fair, and had gone off in a hurry for fear they might be late. Indeed, they had been quite distressed at hearing of Virginia's disappearance, as they were very grateful to Mr. Otis for having allowed them to camp in his park, and four of their number had stayed behind to help in the search. The carp pond had been dragged, and the whole Chase thoroughly gone over, but without any result. It was evident that, for that night at any rate, Virginia was lost to them; and it was in a state of the deepest depression that Mr. Otis and the boys walked up to the house, the groom following behind with the two horses and the pony.

In the hall they found a group of frightened servants, and lying on a sofa in the library was poor Mrs. Otis, almost out of her mind with terror and anxiety, and having her forehead bathed with eau-de-cologne by the old housekeeper. Mr. Otis at once insisted on her having something to eat, and ordered up supper for the whole party. It was a melancholy meal, as hardly anyone spoke, and even the twins were awestruck and subdued, as they were very fond of their sister. When they had finished, Mr. Otis, in spite of the entreaties of the little Duke, ordered them all to bed, saying that nothing more could be done that night, and that he would telegraph in the morning to Scotland Yard for some detectives to be sent down immediately. Just as they were passing out of the dining room, midnight began to boom from the clock tower, and when the last stroke sounded they heard a crash and a sudden shrill cry; a dreadful peal of thunder shook the house, a strain of unearthly music floated through the air, a panel at the top of the staircase flew back with a loud noise, and out on the landing, looking very pale and white, with a little casket in her hand, stepped Virginia. In a moment they had all rushed up to her. Mrs. Otis clasped her passionately in her arms, the Duke smothered her with violent kisses, and the twins executed a wild war dance round the group.

'Good heavens! child, where have you been?' said Mr. Otis, rather angrily, thinking that she had been playing some foolish trick on them. 'Cecil and I have been riding all over the country looking for you, and your mother has been frightened to death. You must never play these practical joks any more.'

'Except on the Ghost! except on the Ghost!' shrieked the twins, as they capered about.

'My own darling, thank God you are found; you must never leave my side again,' murmured Mrs. Otis, as she kissed the trembling child, and smoothed the tangled gold of her hair.

'Papa,' said Virginia quietly, 'I have been with the Ghost. He is dead, and you must come and see him. He had been very wicked, but he was really sorry for all that he had done, and he gave me this box of beautiful jewels before he died.'

The whole family gazed at her in mute amazement, but she was quite grave and serious; and, turning round, she led them through the opening in the wainscoting down a narrow secret corridor, Washington following with a lighted candle, which he had caught up from the table. Finally, they came to a great oak door, studded with rusty nails. When Virginia touched it, it swung back on its heavy hinges, and they found themselves in a little low room, with a vaulted ceiling, and one tiny grated window. Embedded in the wall was a huge iron ring, and chained to it was a gaunt skeleton, that was stretched out at full length on the stone floor, and seemed to be trying to grasp with its long fleshless fingers an old-fashioned trencher and ewer that were placed just out of its reach. The jug had evidently been once filled with water, as it was covered inside with green mould. There was nothing on the trencher but a pile of dust. Virginia knelt down beside the skeleton, and, folding her little hands together, began to pray silently, while the rest of the party looked on in wonder at the terrible tragedy whose secret was now disclosed to them.

'Hallo!' suddenly exclaimed one of the twins, who had been looking out of the window to try and discover in what wing of the house the room was situated. 'Hallo! the old withered almond tree has blossomed. I can see the flowers quite plainly in the moonlight.'

'God has forgiven him,' said Virginia gravely, as

she rose to her feet, and a beautiful light seemed to illumine her face.

'What an angel you are!' cried the young Duke, and he put his arm round her neck, and kissed her.

Four days after these curious incidents a funeral started from Canterville Chase at about eleven o'clock at night. The hearse was drawn by eight black horses, each of which carried on its head a great tuft of nodding ostrich plumes, and the leaden coffin was covered by a rich purple pall, on which was embroidered in gold the Canterville coat-of-arms. By the side of the hearse and the coaches walked the servants with lighted torches, and the whole procession was wonderfully impressive. Lord Canterville was the chief mourner, having come up specially from Wales to attend the funeral, and sat in the first carriage along with little Virginia. Then came the United States Minister and his wife, then Washington and the three boys, and in the last carriage was Mrs. Umney. It was generally felt that as she had been frightened by the ghost for more than fifty years of her life, she had a right to see the last of him. A deep grave had been dug in the corner of the churchyard, just under the old yew-tree, and the service was read in the most impressive manner by the Rev. Augustus Dampier. When the ceremony was over, the servants, according to an old custom observed in the Canterville family, extinguished their torches, and, as the coffin was being lowered into the grave, Virginia stepped forward, and laid on it a large cross made of white and pink almond-blossoms. As she did so, the moon came out from behind a cloud, and flooded with its silent silver the little churchyard, and from a distant copse a nightingale began to sing. She thought of the ghost's description of the Garden of Death, her eyes became dim with tears, and she hardly spoke a word during the drive home.

The next morning, before Lord Canterville went up to town, Mr. Otis had an interview with him on the subject of the jewels the ghost had given to Virginia. They were perfectly magnificent, especially a certain ruby necklace with old Venetian setting, which was really a superb specimen of sixteenth-century work, and their value was so great that Mr. Otis felt considerable scruples about allowing his daughter to accept them.

'My Lord,' he said,' I know that in this country mortmain is held to apply to trinkets as well as to land, and it is quite clear to me that these jewels are, or should be, heirlooms in your family. I must beg you, accordingly, to take them to London with you, and to regard them simply as a portion of your property which has been restored to you under certain strange conditions. As for my daughter, she is merely a child, and has as yet, I am glad to say, but little interest in such appurtenances of idle luxury. I am also informed by Mrs. Otis, who, I may say, is no mean authority upon Art—having had the privilege of spending several winters in Boston when she was a girl—that these gems are of great monetary worth, and if offered for sale would fetch a tall price. Under these circumstances, Lord Canterville, I feel sure that you will recognise how impossible it would be for me to allow them to remain in the possession of any member of my family; and, indeed, all such vain gauds and toys, however suitable or necessary to the dignity of the British aristocracy, would be completely out of place among those who have been brought up on the severe, and I believe immortal, principles of Republican simplicity. Perhaps I should mention that Virginia is very anxious that you should allow her to retain the box, as a memento of your unfortunate but misguided ancestor. As it is extremely old, and consequently a good deal out of repair, you may perhaps think fit to comply with her request. For my own part, I confess I am a good deal surprised to find a child of mine expressing sympathy with mediaevalism in any form, and can only account for it by the fact that Virginia was born in one of your London suburbs shortly after Mrs. Otis had returned from a trip to Athens.'

Lord Canterville listened very gravely to the worthy Minister's speech, pulling his grey moustache now and then to hide an involuntary smile, and when Mr. Otis had ended, he shook him cordially by the hand, and said, 'My dear sir, your charming little daughter rendered my unlucky ancestor, Sir Simon, a very important service, and I and my family are much indebted to her for her marvellous courage and pluck. The jewels are clearly hers, and, egad, I believe that if I were heartless enough to take them from her, the wicked old fellow would be out of his grave in a fortnight, leading me the devil of a life. As for their being heirlooms, nothing is an heirloom that is not so mentioned in a will or legal document, and the existence of these jewels has been quite unknown. I assure you I have no more claim on them than your butler, and when Miss Virginia grows up I daresay she will be pleased to have pretty things to wear. Besides, you forget, Mr. Otis, that you took the furniture and the ghost at a valuation, and anything that belonged to the ghost passed at once into your possession, as whatever activity Sir Simon may have shown in the corridor at night, in point of law he was really dead, and you acquired his property by purchase.'

Mr. Otis was a good deal distressed at Lord Canterville's refusal, and begged him to reconsider his decision, but the good-natured peer was quite firm, and finally induced the Minister to allow his daughter to retain the present the ghost had given her, and when, in the spring of 1890, the young Duchess of Cheshire was presented at the Queen's first drawing room on the occasion of her marriage, her jewels were the universal theme of admiration. For Virginia received the coronet, which is the reward of all good little American girls, and was married to her boy-lover as soon as he came of age. They were both so charming, and they loved each other so much, that every one was delighted at the match, except the old Marchioness of Dumbleton, who had tried to catch the Duke for one of her seven unmarried daughters, and had given no less than three expensive dinner parties for that purpose, and, strange to say, Mr. Otis himself. Mr. Otis was extremely fond of the young Duke personally, but, theoretically, he objected to titles, and, to use his own words, 'was not without apprehension lest, amid the enervating influences of a pleasure-loving aristocracy, the true principles of Republican simplicity should be forgotten.' His objections, however, were completely overruled, and I believe that when he walked up the aisle of St. George's, Hanover Square, with his daughter leaning on his arm, there was not a prouder man in the whole length and breadth of England.

The Duke and Duchess, after the honeymoon, went down to Canterville Chase, and on the day after their arrival they walked over in the afternoon to the lonely churchyard. There had been a great deal of difficulty at first about the inscription on Sir Simon's tombstone, but finally it had been decided to engrave on it simply the initials of the old gentleman's name, and the verse from the library window. The Duchess had brought with her some lovely roses, which she strewed upon the grave, and after they had stood by it for some time, they strolled into the ruined chancel of the old abbey. There the Duchess sat down on a fallen pillar, while her husband lay at her feet smoking a cigarette and looking up at her beautiful eyes. Suddenly he threw his cigarette away, took hold of her hand, and said to her, 'Virginia, a wife should have no secrets from her husband.

'Dear Cecil! I have no secrets from you.'

'Yes, you have,' he answered, smiling, 'you have never told me what happened to you when you were locked up with the ghost.'

'I have never told anyone, Cecil,' said Virginia gravely.

'I know that, but you might tell me.'

'Please don't ask me, Cecil, I cannot tell you. Poor Sir Simon! I owe him a great deal. Yes, don't laugh, Cecil, I really do. He made me see what Life is, and what Death signifies, and why Love is stronger than both.' The Duke rose and kissed his wife lovingly.

'You can have your secret as long as I have your heart,' he murmured.

'You have always had that, Cecil.'

About the Author

Oscar Wilde (1854-1900) was an Irish writer and poet. He became one of London's most popular playwrights in the early 1890s.

John Mortonson's Funeral

Ambrose Bierce

When John Mortonson was dead his lines in 'the tragedy 'Man" had all been spoken and he had left the stage.

The body rested in a fine mahogany coffin fitted with a plate of glass. All arrangements for the funeral had been so well attended to that had the deceased known, he would doubtless have approved. The face, as it showed under the glass, was not disagreeable to look upon: it bore a faint smile, and as the death had been painless, had not been distorted beyond the repairing power of the undertaker. At two o'clock of the afternoon, the friends were to assemble to pay their last tribute of respect to one who had no further need of friends and respect. The surviving members of the family came severally every few minutes to the casket and wept above the placid features beneath the glass. This did them no good; it did no good to John Mortonson; but in the presence of death, reason and philosophy are silent.

As the hour of two approached, the friends began to arrive and after offering such consolation to the stricken relatives as the proprieties of the occasion required, solemnly seated themselves about the room with an augmented consciousness of their importance in the scheme funereal. Then the minister came, and in that overshadowing presence the lesser lights went into eclipse. His entrance was followed by that of the widow, whose lamentations filled the room. She approached the casket and after leaning her face against the cold glass for a moment, was gently led to a seat near her daughter. Mournfully and low, the man of God began his eulogy of the dead, and his doleful voice, mingled with the sobbing which it was its purpose to stimulate and sustain, rose and fell, seemed to come and go, like the sound of a sullen sea. The gloomy day grew darker as he spoke; a curtain of cloud underspread the sky and a few drops of rain fell audibly. It seemed as if all nature were weeping for John Mortonson.

When the minister had finished his eulogy with prayer, a hymn was sung and the pall-bearers took their places beside the bier. As the last notes of the hymn died away, the widow ran to the coffin, cast herself upon it and sobbed hysterically. Gradually, however, she yielded to dissuasion, becoming more composed; and as the minister was in the act of leading her away, her eyes sought the face of the dead beneath the glass. She threw up her arms and with a shriek fell backward insensible.

The mourners sprang forward to the coffin, the friends followed, and as the clock on the mantel solemnly struck three all were staring down upon the face of John Mortonson, deceased.

They turned away, sick and faint. One man, trying in his terror to escape the awful sight, stumbled against the coffin so heavily as to knock away one of its frail supports. The coffin fell to the floor, the glass was shattered to bits by the concussion.

From the opening crawled John Mortonson's cat, which lazily leapt to the floor, sat up, tranquilly wiped its crimson muzzle with a forepaw, then walked with dignity from the room.

About the Author

Ambrose Bierce (June 24, 1842 - sometime after December 26, 1913) was an American journalist, short story writer, fabulist, and satirist. In 1913, Bierce travelled to Mexico to gain first-hand experience of the Mexican Revolution. While travelling with rebel troops, he disappeared without a trace.

Glossary

Apprised: To make aware of.

Arroyos: The dry bed of a stream.

Bugle: A brass wind instrument resembling a cornet and sometimes having keys or valves, used typically for sounding military signals.

Collegiate: Of or pertaining to a college.

Condescending: To behave as if one is conscious of descending from a superior position, rank, or dignity.

Contorted: Twisted in a violent manner; distorted

Deplorable: To be very sorry about....

Disposition: The predominant or prevailing tendency of one's spirits; natural mental and emotional outlook or mood; characteristic attitude.

Intrepidity: An act that goes beyond the limits set by a moral principle, standard, low etc.

Petrified: To turn into stone.

Reproached: To find fault with a person.

Transgression: Great bravery.

Vassal: In the European feudal system.

Vaudeville: A threatrical entertainment featuring a variety of acts.